Beth canno

"This was my chance to work with a big newspaper in a big city. How good that would look on a résumé. Well, I'll tell you. I'd rather rot in Henderson than stay one minute longer with people who have deceived me. Were all the questions for the column planted?"

Without waiting for an answer, she plunged on. "All of you need truth in your lives. If you go easy on Jesus, you go easy on the truth. I wish I'd never come here. I wish I'd never seen any of you. I can't stand it. I just can't stand it."

Aunt Catherine and Ross moved as if to come to her. "No, don't touch me," Beth said and put her hand out as a shield. "Get away."

She didn't feel like herself anymore. And according to Aunt Catherine, she wasn't. . . Something deep inside was spilling over—just as the tears were now spilling from her eyes—and she seemed helpless to prevent either flood from happening.

"I thought all of you were the most wonderful people I'd ever met. You were good and honorable and in positions of power and influence. I've never liked the jokes about politicians. I never believed the majority of public-office holders were crooked and out for themselves.

"Now I discover that the people who set the best example weren't real. You all were wearing very attractive masks. I never want to see any of you again. I'm going home. Where I belong."

Jacobs got up and left the room. Ross walked over to a window, staring out. "Let me go with you," Aunt Catherine said. "Or help you pack. Just let me explain."

"It's a little late for explanations. And as for packing, there's nothing here I want. The biggest celebration in Henderson is a cookout for the city council candidates. I wear blue jeans to that."

YVONNE LEHMAN, an award-winning novelist, lives in the heart of North Carolina's Smoky Mountains with her husband. They are the parents of four grown children. In addition to being an inspirational romance writer, she is also the founder of the Blue Ridge Christian Writers' Conference.

HEARTSONG PRESENTS

Books by Yvonne Lehman

HP37—Drums of Shelomoh
HP82—Southern Gentleman
HP126—Mountain Man
HP201—A Whole New World
HP218—Hawaiian Heartbeat
HP290—After the Storm
HP305—Call of the Mountain
HP338—Somewhere a Rainbow
HP357—Whiter Than Snow
HP373—Catch of a Lifetime

Secret
Ballot

Yvonne Lehman

Heartsong Presents

A note from the author:
*I love to hear from my readers! You may correspond with me
by writing:* **Yvonnne Lehman**
Author Relations
PO Box 719
Uhrichsville, OH 44683

ISBN 1-58660-066-4

SECRET BALLOT

Cover design by Robyn Martins.

PRINTED IN THE U.S.A.

one

If Bob had given her an engagement ring for Christmas instead of a bottle of perfume, Beth Simmons was certain she would be planning her wedding rather than considering Aunt Catherine's invitation to see something of the world. Her aunt had it all arranged. Beth would arrive in Washington, D.C., during the last week in March and spend two months there. She would live in the Rossiters' Victorian mansion. Since Beth had been a journalism major and was writing for the local paper, she would write Catherine's "Ask Auntie" advice column in the newspaper owned by Senator Rossiter and help Catherine's assistant society editor.

In June, she would return to Henderson, South Carolina, and spend the summer with Bob, who would be on vacation from his teaching job. Beth would have had her adventure. She could then settle down and marry. Surely her leaving for a couple of months would inspire Bob to reconsider purchasing the long-awaited ring. He would realize that absence makes the heart grow fonder.

Beth removed the stopper from the bottle of perfume and waved it beneath her nose. The scent was nice. So was Bob. Everyone said so. And the Christmas gift hadn't been a disappointment, exactly. It didn't change their plans to marry someday. Bob was just being sensible to wait until he could afford a ring without going into debt. But she so wished that Bob would once, just once, do

5

something that was not predictable and sensible.

She supposed she had a touch of Aunt Catherine in her. There was no doubt she and Bob were right for each other. She'd never felt so compatible with anyone else. Her parents approved of Bob, describing him as "dependable, reliable, practical." Being tall and athletic, Bob had been a basketball star in college. Now he taught history and coached at the elementary school. His blond good looks caused many women to look his way. But he'd faithfully kept his attention on Beth during the past two years.

Her glance fell upon the mantle clock: 11:55. In another five minutes Christmas Day would be gone. There hadn't been any snow, just cold wind and a clear sky. Beth's parents had conveniently said good night after she and Bob came home from the church Christmas program. Now she and Bob sat on the couch in the downstairs family room, looking at the flames in the fireplace that were slowly dying. Beth gazed at the lighted tree. The lights were small ones, blinking on and off. She wondered if Aunt Catherine were looking at the tree on the White House lawn—from the inside.

Feeling the movement of Bob's arm around her shoulders, Beth's thoughts returned to the situation at hand. She lifted the perfume to her nose, then turned her face toward Bob.

She smiled. "I love the scent."

"And I love you," he said, his face very close to hers.

Normally, she would have drawn nearer for his kiss. But instead, she drew in a deep breath and then spoke. "Aunt Catherine wants me to go to Washington."

He moved his arm from around her shoulders. "That's no surprise. She's wanted that for several years." Leaning forward, he touched the engraved nameplate Beth had given him for Christmas. Beth looked at it. It was for his desk at school. Like him, it was very handsome—Robert G. Johnson.

Her voice was low. "But this time I'm going." Her gaze went to the Christmas tree lights again, and it crossed her mind that flashing lights meant danger. The feeling inside her was not fear, however, but exhilaration. "Even my parents are encouraging it."

The fire burned lower and was almost out. Bob walked over to the fireplace and stood with his back to it. He didn't say, "Don't go." He just said, "When are you going?"

Beth swallowed hard. Of course he couldn't ask that she not go. They weren't officially engaged yet. "She wants me there by the last week in March."

Bob nodded and straightened, making his tall frame even taller. He shoved his hands deep into his pockets, a gesture he often did when he didn't know what else to do. He rocked gently on the soles of his shoes. "And how long do you plan to be gone?"

Beth shrugged. "A few weeks." She could have said, "Nine, to be exact." Aunt Catherine had specified two months—plus the last week of March.

After a brief silence Bob spoke. "I know you have always wanted to visit with your aunt Catherine. You'd probably regret it later if you didn't." His smile was sweet, but his eyes spoke of a sadness his lips did not utter.

Beth felt mixed emotions. She longed for Bob to say he couldn't live without her and didn't want her to be away from him for two months. At the same time, she knew he was right—she would regret it all her life if she didn't accept this invitation from her aunt, who was the most exciting woman she'd ever known. Bob was just unselfishly thinking of Beth.

"I know you're extrabusy near the end of the school year," she said defensively. "I'll be back the first of June. We'll have all summer together."

Beth set the perfume on the coffee table, went over to Bob, and he enfolded her in his arms. His lips came down on hers. She always felt loved and secure in his arms. They both had agreed there would be no sex outside of marriage, but somehow there never seemed to be enough of anything for her—enough of Bob, enough challenge at the newspaper, enough excitement in the small town of Henderson. Perhaps that was because she'd always compared Henderson with Washington, the dullness of her own life with the excitement of Aunt Catherine's.

❧

After Bob left, Beth placed the screen around the fireplace, unplugged the Christmas tree lights, and went to her bedroom, adjacent to the family room. She always felt slightly depressed after Christmas, when the birth of Christ had been celebrated, the presents had been opened, the guests had gone, and the parties were over.

But as she thought of Aunt Catherine's letter, anticipation and excitement began to creep over her. Lying in bed in warm flannel pajamas, Beth read the letter again:

Darling,
  You must help me out. I have the chance to be off to the Caribbean. I need someone to take my place for the "Ask Auntie" advice column. You can also assist my assistant society editor. Also, my boss, who incidentally owns the newspaper, is looking for someone

*to type some memoirs for him. You would live in his
house.*

*In case anyone is worried about that, tell them that
everything is perfectly legitimate. Jacobs, the
Rossiters' editor/political advisor will live in the
house while you're there, as well as a couple who
looks after the house. Several other employees come
in when needed.*

*This is your chance, Beth! Give yourself a little
adventure before you settle down with that school-
teacher of yours.*

*Love,
Aunt Catherine*

Beth smiled. She could almost hear Aunt Catherine
talking. Strange, how different sisters could be. Beth's
own mother was a demure, sensible woman, who was
attractive but always wanting to shed fifteen to twenty
pounds. She kept her medium brown hair cut short for
easy handling. Her eyes were a clear blue, and her oval
face looked younger than her fifty-two years. Beth was
named after her: Mary Elizabeth Simmons.

Her mother said Aunt Catherine's hair was dyed, but
Beth didn't mind that. No different-colored roots ever
showed during the few times Catherine had visited. Her
copper-color hair held golden highlights, and she usually
wore it piled high in an elaborate chignon with swooping
waves around her beautiful face.

Catherine's eyes were catlike green, and she knew how
to apply makeup to her advantage. She was forty-eight
years old, but she looked to be at least ten years younger
than Beth's mother. Beth was pleased that her own hips,

like Catherine's, were trim, and she determined to keep them that way with daily exercise.

Suddenly, laying the letter aside, Beth jumped from the bed and stood in front of the mirror, appraising herself. Lifting strands of her hair, she smirked. Auburn, with only a trace of golden sheen if in strong light. Leaning forward, she peered at her eyes. Shaped like Aunt Catherine's, yes. But the color was light gray. Then she said aloud to her reflection, "Aunt Catherine, Washington, cherry blossoms, dining with diplomats, tea on the White House lawn."

She smiled, transforming her face. It was possible to bring life to those dull gray eyes. They held a trace of green then—with envy, no doubt, of the delightful lifestyle lived by her aunt. She wondered if Bob saw them sparkle after he had kissed her. She wondered if they had sparkled then.

Sighing, she went back to bed and picked up the letter. "Your coming the last week in March will give us time to get you settled in. I leave on my cruise to the Caribbean April 1, so please don't let me down, Beth. I'm counting on you."

Beth hoped she wasn't being an April fool, leaving Bob for two months. But she quickly justified her intentions by reminding herself they were not officially engaged—just verbally promised. And let Aunt Catherine down? That was the last thing Beth ever wanted to do. Catherine had invited her to visit before, but this was the first time she had ever asked such a favor. She wanted Beth to assist the society editor. That really shouldn't be difficult, considering the reporting Beth had done on serious matters such as the homeless, burned-out businesses, and shootings.

Writing the "Ask Auntie" column should be a breeze.

Taking a scrapbook from a bookshelf, Beth opened to the columns she'd pasted. She laughed at some, empathized with others, and looked forward to trying her hand at answering similar questions.

After reading several pages, Beth yawned and closed the scrapbook. She had always looked upon Catherine as having the ideal life of glamour and travel. Of course, Beth knew a right relationship with God was most important. But couldn't one be a dedicated Christian and still have an exciting life, enjoying the world God had created?

She intended to find out.

With the lamp still aglow next to the scrapbook, Beth lay back on her pillow and gazed toward the ceiling, thoughtful. Aunt Catherine had been inviting her to visit during cherry blossom time ever since Beth entered college, but it never came at the same time as spring break. Her parents had said she needed to work during the summer for school clothes, although it had been Aunt Catherine who supplied the money for her college tuition. Beth's father, being a pharmacist and having no other children, could well afford it, but Catherine had insisted they let her do at least that much for her niece.

This time when the invitation arrived, there had been no excuse from her parents. They looked sad when they said it but agreed that the time had come for Beth to make this journey away from Henderson. Perhaps they wanted her to see firsthand that their warnings through the years—all that glitters isn't gold—applied to Catherine's lifestyle.

Beth, at age twenty-five, was aware of that. Yet she needed to get this wandering urge out of her system before she settled down with Bob. She glanced at the bottle of perfume and realized again how the gift had clinched her decision to go to Washington. More than ever, she realized the truth of the last line of her aunt's letter: *If you don't come now, you never will.*

ॐ

Now or never kept running through Catherine McKelvey's mind, day in and day out. She hoped she wasn't making another mistake. Goodness knows, she'd made enough of them in her lifetime. But Beth's visit had been agreed upon by the three of them: Mary Elizabeth, John, and herself. However, Mary and John didn't know all the reasons.

Catherine fluttered around in her apartment in the Capitol House, where she served as hostess to many events, including entertaining foreign dignitaries. Beth had always thought she lived such a glamorous life. Catherine had tried to make it sound glamorous. But now Beth would see firsthand.

She touched her perfectly groomed, flame-colored hair as she gazed into a mirror. Green eyes stared at her—not with confidence, but with trepidation.

Even though Mary and John had agreed to this, Catherine wondered if they'd done it because they thought it right, or if her persistence had worn them down. They were good people. They wanted to do right. They were led by God.

That thought stabbed Catherine's heart. How different she was from Mary and John. She lived in an entirely different world. It was time Beth knew something about that world. And in any event, second thoughts she might have about this visit were coming too late. Time was speeding by, and in less than three months, Beth would arrive in Washington; and Catherine's carefully laid plans would be put into effect.

"Yes," Catherine said aloud, trying to erase the doubt in

the green eyes staring back at her from the mirror. "The time has come for Beth to spread her wings."

Or get them clipped came her reflection's unbidden response.

two

The package was hand-delivered.

Jacob L. Jacobs, editor in chief of the *Washingtonian Times* and political advisor to Senator Clement R. Rossiter II and C. Ross Rossiter III, stared at the manila envelope, remembering Catherine's words: "Beth is a small-town girl, deeply religious, sheltered, in love with a fine young man, and I expect you to see that she remains as sweet as she is when she arrives in Washington."

He ran his middle-aged fingers over his closely cropped, dark hair that held a sprinkling of gray at his temples, and he thought of Catherine's words. He had mixed feelings about them.

What kind of implication was Catherine making? Was it a dig alluding to his own younger years of an unsavory past? Or was she implying that he should keep an eye on Ross, who had a roving eye for pretty girls and a reputation of being a charmer with a penchant to love 'em and leave 'em?

Being a well-accomplished matchmaker, could it be possible that Catherine hoped that Beth would be the one to capture Ross's heart? Surely she wouldn't take that chance with her own niece.

He knew Catherine had never married, but she certainly wasn't a naïve woman—especially after having survived so many years in the nation's capital. He wondered what Catherine's real reasons might be for taking a two-month trip and leaving her niece with him and Ross. If going to the Caribbean was so important, why didn't she go before April?

Or was her reason so personal she didn't want to talk about it?

Jacobs shrugged away his questions, and his scowl turned into a grin. This was just part of Catherine's charm. If ever there was an unpredictable lady, it was she. Catherine could not be put in a box. That's one reason she'd been asked, years ago, to be hostess at Capitol House, welcoming dignitaries and supervising dinners for the White House. Her personality made others feel they were the most important people around—at least, it made most people feel that way.

But this was not a time to think about Catherine. He'd been stymied by her actions before. All the contemplation in the world didn't bring the answers. With renewed determination he released the clasp on the envelope and took out the papers. As he expected, the report was brief—only two pages.

The report was a routine check made on all employees for about the past fifteen years, ever since a young reporter for the newspaper had sent threatening letters to the White House and later they'd discovered he'd had a history of mental instability.

Some critics had asked the question, "Why didn't Senator Rossiter know about that?"

The question had a way of placing doubt on the credibility of Senator Rossiter, whose family had owned the paper for several generations. The implication was that since the senator and the president belonged to different political parties, then perhaps the reporter's actions hadn't been as simply explained as it appeared. Had the senator had some hand in the incident?

Once such a spark of distrust was planted, it wasn't easy to overcome. Fortunately, the senator was the son of a revered former ambassador, and his record and character were impeccable. His constituents, and even some from the opposing party, refused to let the sparks of innuendo burst into a full-fledged firestorm.

Since then, Jacobs had felt it imperative to have a background check on each employee who had been with the paper less than five years and every new one, even if that employee was a temporary two-month replacement and the niece of Catherine McKelvey, whom he'd known for more than twenty-five years.

Jacobs smiled as he read over the information that told him no more than he'd expected. The young woman had been a good student through school, graduated with honors at an area college where she had majored in journalism, worked with the local newspaper for three years, was a member of the First Church where she sang in the choir, and still lived with her parents.

Then something caught his eye.

Jacobs read it over three times.

After a thoughtful moment, he shrugged. He supposed this wasn't anyone else's business. After reading the information one more time, he slipped the papers back into the envelope and walked over to a file cabinet. He found no reason why Mary Elizabeth Simmons shouldn't fill in temporarily for Catherine McKelvey.

And too, he found no reason to divulge the information he had just filed away—despite its having been rather thought-provoking. And no, it wasn't anything that either of the Rossiters needed to know. It was not of any criminal or threatening nature.

But it was surprising, nonetheless, that Catherine hadn't mentioned that particular bit of history.

Why not?

≥∘

Ross Rossiter didn't have time to be concerned about Catherine's telling him—not asking, but telling him—that she would be in the Caribbean for two months and her niece would substitute for her. That didn't concern him, because it was Jacobs's job to see that all ran well with the newspaper when Ross wasn't around. He never gave much thought to the "Ask Auntie" column, considering it to be a rather frivolous thing women liked. It was a popular part of the paper, so he left it alone. And it was no concern of his what the White House did about a hostess for the Capitol House while Catherine was gone.

He would miss Catherine. She was a bright spot on the Washington scene and a family friend after having devoted her time to the newspaper for more than two decades. Maybe she thought she'd groom her niece to take over when she retired.

Catherine retire? Ross couldn't image the dynamic Catherine ever retiring. She seemed ageless. Maybe Catherine, the matchmaker, had something else in mind.

Ross smiled at that. On occasion he'd jokingly said he wished Catherine herself were twenty years younger or he twenty years older and they'd paint the town red. Both had laughed. If she hadn't laughed, Ross could easily have forgotten such a beautiful and charming woman's age. However, Catherine treated him like a son—one she didn't mind scolding when she felt he'd been behaving in an inappropriate manner.

He had been seen around town with some winsome

daughters of politicians and quite a few film stars. But if this young niece of hers had an inkling of Catherine's looks and abilities, Ross could find her very interesting.

Yes, very interesting indeed. So, Catherine was up to some kind of matchmaking scheme, eh? Well, if this girl was anything like Catherine, he wouldn't mind. He wouldn't mind at all.

three

The longest two months of Beth's life were January and February. Then March dragged on forever as she made plans to leave for Washington. Her call to Aunt Catherine late in the month revealed that snow was being forecast for the day Beth planned to arrive in Washington. Beth's heart skipped a beat. Snow rarely fell on Henderson. Of course Washington would have snow. Washington had everything!

Although she was too excited to eat, she looked at the big breakfast her mother had prepared the morning of her departure. Beth was scheduled to leave in the afternoon. Sighing at the amount of food placed before her, she determined she would try to eat. Otherwise her parents would worry. They had agreed with this trip, but both of them had also seemed to try and find every reason she shouldn't go.

Maybe she'd waited too long to cut the cord. She'd lived at home all of her twenty-five years. It was more convenient and less expensive while going to Furman University, only twenty miles away. Then after she graduated and got a job with the local newspaper, her paternal grandparents had died in a car crash. Her mom's parents had died when Beth was still a young girl. With both sets of grandparents gone, it seemed she and her family needed each other more than ever, and there'd been no mention of Beth moving out. She hadn't wanted to live alone in some apartment.

19

"What about your position with the paper, Beth?" her father asked, as if he were having second thoughts about her leaving. "You said the editor can't guarantee you'll have a job when you return."

That did not daunt Beth's spirit one iota. "Dad, two months with a Washington paper is more recommendation than a lifetime with the *Henderson News*. You know that. I don't want to be stuck with this paper all my life. I have a degree in journalism. I need some kind of experience behind me before any magazine or larger paper will hire me."

He peered at her through his dark-rimmed eyeglasses. "That may be true. And I know your aunt Catherine has made Washington seem like the most glamorous place in the world," he said quietly—*almost like a stranger would talk,* Beth thought. "But there are some pretty rough things that go on there. You devour those papers daily. You know what I mean."

Beth nodded her head in agreement but determined not to be swayed. She'd never gone against her parents' wishes. She'd never even had that rebellious streak that was supposed to be so common between parents and teenagers. She'd been raised to honor her parents, and they had respected her.

She knew their reluctance to have her go was not because they were narrow-minded. Rather the opposite. They were well aware of the dangers in what they called "the world out there," as if Henderson somehow was not a part of it. She was inclined to agree with them.

"Honey," her mother added softly, "you'll only be writing an advice column. Something like 'Dear Abby.' "

Surprise washed over Beth. She'd often felt her mother

tried to shield her from Aunt Catherine's influence, trying to make her content with her life as it was in Henderson, but her mother was not one to come out and make any derogatory statement about anyone. This was the closest she had ever come.

"Mom, don't you know that 'Dear Abby' has been a very popular syndicated column for years?"

"Of course, dear. I'm not saying there's anything wrong with it. But. . .can such a column really further your career?"

"It depends on what one puts in the column, Mom. You've taught me well, don't you think?"

Beth grinned, and her mother's reserve melted as she nodded with a look of love and acceptance on her face. "I guess we have to let you go. . .sometime."

Now is the time, insisted part of Beth's mind, contending with her desire to please her parents. But she had to defend her dream city. "Dad," she said, glancing at him but not looking steadily into his eyes, which she knew would hold only love and concern for her, "I know there are dangers out there. But Washington is also the symbol of all that is great and wonderful about our nation. It's where some of the most important decisions in the world are made. I know patriotism isn't always popular today, but I'm a natural flag-waver. I love my country. I love what Washington represents." She added reluctantly, "It's not just Aunt Catherine."

Although her parents had never said it in so many words, she knew they didn't quite approve of Catherine.

Beth's father furrowed his brow. "We just don't want you hurt, honey."

"Hurt?" she exclaimed, looking from one parent to the

other. "You two act like it's the end of the world."

"You're the biggest part of our world, Beth," her dad said. "And you're our child, no matter how old you get."

He lowered his eyes to his plate and looked so dejected that Beth reached out and touched his hand. "Dad," she said softly, "it's only about three hours away by plane. If anything went wrong I could call you at lunchtime and be back here before supper."

After an uncomfortable silence her mother asked, "What does Bob think about your going away for two months?"

"He said I would probably regret it if I didn't."

Her mother nodded and pushed her food around her plate.

Beth felt sure her trip to Washington didn't call for such dramatics from her parents. Trying to be cheerful, she added lightly, "Anyway, Bob says my gorgeous diamond ring will be on my finger by summer, and the wedding is still on for. . .the future."

They both looked at her. Beth lowered her eyes to her plate and forced a bite of cold eggs into her mouth. She wondered if her eyes had sparkled when she spoke of her someday-wedding. Or did they sparkle only when she spoke of Washington and Aunt Catherine?

"I know you expect a lot, Beth," her mother said finally. "But glamour soon wears thin. It's the routine daily existence that makes the world go round."

Beth believed that, but it didn't make her like it.

"Besides," her mother continued, "it could be rather dull without Catherine there."

Beth had the feeling they were glad Catherine was not going to be in Washington during most of her visit. But that city could never be dull. And she would be there in time for the famous cherry blossom season.

❧

That afternoon, after her parents said a reluctant good-bye at the airport, Beth looked down at the sea of clouds, foam-like in great feathery swills, light, suspended in space. The great flying machine seemed to be the only movable object in the universe. Far below, spread out in perfect order, lay a huge map where inhabitants and even vehicles were too small to be seen.

She leaned back in the seat, not inclined to disturb the man next to her, who was reading a magazine. She smiled and closed her eyes, secure that her life was completely in God's hands. Everyone knew a big thing like this plane, carrying 250 people, couldn't fly. Then again, neither could the bumblebee. But God had a way of making the impossible possible.

The bumblebee did fly. And with the cooperation of many human beings, so did this airplane. But when it came right down to the nitty-gritty, she knew that only God could pilot a plane. Only He could keep it in the air. That's why she loved to fly. At a time like this, doing the impossible, having no control whatsoever over her circumstances, she felt her faith was strongest, and her life rested completely in God's hands.

four

What Beth expected to be an exciting week with Catherine turned out to be an enchanted lifetime. A world in Washington was a different world, or was it just that Catherine made it seem so? From the moment Beth stepped out of the plane at Ronald Reagan Washington National and into the limousine with Aunt Catherine, the conversation was different from any she'd ever had.

Her itinerary was laid out as if she were a visiting celebrity, and all of Washington were waiting to receive her. Catherine even had it printed out—appointments, shopping, dinners—and just hearing the talk of it made Beth feel breathless, as if she were Cinderella getting ready for the dance of her lifetime.

Aunt Catherine had an apartment on the second floor of the Capitol House, consisting of a lavish bedroom, small kitchenette, sitting room, small alcove library, and a bathroom larger than Beth's bedroom back home. The first floor contained the living room, dining room, an expansive foyer separating those two rooms, and a kitchen that any restaurant would envy. She could well understand how dignitaries would be impressed when entertained there. On the third floor were guest bedrooms. Aunt Catherine offered Beth her pick of those rooms, but she opted to sleep in her aunt's sitting room where the couch opened into a queen-sized bed.

After getting into their nighties, the two women propped

up against plush pillows and talked about everything under the sun until the wee hours of the morning. Aunt Catherine said not to worry about it. They could sleep in the next morning as long as they liked.

Beth felt she didn't need sleep. The adrenaline was flowing like an open fire hydrant through her veins. Aunt Catherine seemed as eager as she to start the day, so by ten o'clock the next morning, both women were ready to walk out onto the scuff of snow that softly blanketed the ground and into the brisk March wind that blew all cares away.

Aunt Catherine walked right out onto the sidewalk, stepped onto the curb, and waved her arms like a fairy godmother might when casting a spell to turn a pumpkin into a coach. Magically the coach appeared in the form of a Yellow cab and they were on their way.

"Tonight you meet the Rossiters, the *Washingtonian Times* people you'll be working with, and many, many more who I'm sure you've read about or seen on TV," Beth's aunt explained. She leaned over, making her voice lower, "And some who are never in the limelight but control things with their pocketbooks."

Before Beth could even think how to respond or ask if the president himself would be there, her aunt began talking about pink.

"Pink? Aunt Catherine, I can't imagine me in. . .pink!"

"Trust me, my dear." Her aunt patted her hand reassuringly. "With your coloring, you'll look fabulous in pink. I always get compliments when I wear pink. It's terrific with red hair."

"You would look terrific in a tow sack," Beth retorted. "I can't imagine you looking any other way."

Catherine laughed delightedly. "I knew I asked you up

here for some reason." She hugged Beth's shoulders. "You've always liked me, haven't you?"

That question surprised Beth. She wouldn't have thought of her aunt in terms of ever wondering if someone liked her. She was a free spirit. "I've always loved you, Aunt Catherine. No one is as. . ." She searched for a word and settled on, "colorful."

Catherine's gaze flew to the top of the cab, before giving Beth a side glance. "You're so kind, dear. Now, let's get your hair done first."

&

Beth could hardly believe a blunt cut to right above her shoulders could make such a difference in her appearance. She'd always parted her hair in the middle and let it fall in its natural wave to her shoulders. But Catherine's hairstylist brushed Beth's thick hair from the right side and let it fall along the left side, with a trace of bangs swept toward the left.

"Tres beau," exclaimed Philippe, the stylist, while standing behind her and looking delighted. Aunt Catherine looked on with smug approval, as if she'd known all along.

Strange, how something like sweeping the hair to one side could make a difference. *Viva la difference,* Beth thought, looking at the amber-colored highlights on her hair that had never looked so shiny and soft. The new style seemed utterly natural, although Philippe had brushed out her waves and simply given the ends a slight turn under.

"I love it," she said. Somehow the new style caused her gray eyes to look even larger. Or maybe it was just that emerald gleam in them that made them seem so.

An hour later she stood in a women's clothing shop, staring at the reflection of herself dressed in pink. The soft material was beautiful, and she could do nothing more than admit she looked like her fairy godmother had turned her into some kind of Cinderella. Aunt Catherine chose maroon evening shoes with a strap of rhinestones and a matching bag that she said would go perfectly with a satin-lined maroon wool cape that she had at home in her closet.

Beth continued to stare. The image was more than Cinderella. She was seeing herself as others might see her, and the image was not of a girl, but of a woman. A woman whom Beth wasn't sure she'd ever met before, but whom she looked forward to getting to know.

She was Cinderella being primed by her fairy godmother. She was a princess going to the royal ball. For the first time, she could understand how the original Cinderella, transformed into a lovely woman, could have forgotten that a clock would dare sound a discordant stroke at midnight.

The evening finally came. Even before they entered the Capital Hilton Hotel, Beth was being introduced to lovely people in formal attire. In a span of ten minutes, she smiled, shook hands, and said "Glad to meet you" more than she had ever done in her entire life.

"She looks just like you, Catherine," was the finest compliment Beth could wish for. It was said over and over. Beth began to believe she was that fairy-tale princess. However, she also began to understand why her parents had said her aunt did not live in the real world. Deep inside, Beth was well aware of the stroke of midnight that would inevitably come.

But for now, she would enjoy the dance.

◆

"I've got to meet that one, now," Ross Rossiter mumbled to Jacobs as he stepped back from a table and stared across the crowded room. Normally, until after the speeches were finished, Ross would only greet those closest to him or those who came up to him for a word. The rest of the night could be spent socializing, once the dinner and its related business were completed.

Jacobs knew the moment that Ross saw her. The young man's face became like a still frame for a moment, as if there were a glitch in a movie reel and everything stopped. The pause lasted only a second, for Ross was well-trained in hiding all emotions—a necessary quality for an aspiring politician.

But Jacobs knew Ross well. He followed him across the room, as they shook hands and spoke all along the way, inevitably easing closer to the beauty whose cape was being taken, leaving her looking like cherry blossom time had already come to Washington in all its glory and that the blooms had never appeared so entrancing.

Part of Jacobs's duties were, when the time approached, to remind Ross that he should take his seat at the speakers' table. He often had to advise him that his every adverse action, every impression, every word would someday come back to haunt him if he went into politics. Ross learned easily, perhaps by growing up with a dad who had been a senator for more than twenty years. Jacobs wasn't sure if that were a good quality in the young man or something to be regretted.

Nevertheless, he knew Ross and knew that first glance at Catherine and her young niece fulfilled all the clichés— Ross took to her like a duck to water, like a child to candy, like a match to a gas burner.

Jacobs saw it. He saw the look on Ross's face, the gleam in his eyes, the smile on his lips, the welcome in his handshake, and the forward leaning of his body language. He liked the girl. He found her attractive. But Jacobs would have known that, even if he hadn't been watching for Ross's reaction. Mary Elizabeth Simmons was a young replica of Catherine McKelvey.

❧

"Don't tell me—let me guess," Ross said, walking up to Catherine and the young beauty, who seemed to be swathed in some kind of glow. Maybe this was a dream. But she looked better than any dream he'd ever had. Little Miss Small-Town Girl, Mary Elizabeth Simmons, was actually a charming southern belle who reminded him of magnolias and peach blossoms, although he'd never seen either of those items in person. Maybe the young woman could be convinced to educate him.

"You're the new 'Auntie' who is going to advise all of Washington on how to deal with their problems," he said as he turned from her aunt to greet the newcomer.

Her wide smile, framing perfect white teeth, melted his heart. "I'm going to try, but I may have to ask Aunt Catherine for advice before I send it to the paper."

"I'm sure you'll do fine," Ross said, extending his hand, making his own introduction. Sometimes one couldn't wait for protocol. "I'm Ross Rossiter, and you could be none other than Catherine's niece."

Her smile was accompanied by sparkling eyes that held a trace of green. "I'm Beth," she said. "I'm pleased to meet you, Senator."

"Senator?" Ross tore his eyes away from her and looked at Catherine. But his glance didn't seem able to stray far from this girl for very long. "The senator is my dad— Clement R. Rossiter. I'm his son, the newspaper publisher. Your direct supervisor, however, is Jacobs. He's. . ."

Ross expected Jacobs to be beside him or right behind him but discovered that his mentor and friend had turned away to speak with someone else. Catherine had wandered off in the opposite direction, charming the guests as usual. It sounded as if Catherine had omitted a little information. This lovely young woman seemed not to know about him. But that was all right. She would be living in his home for two months. He hoped they would get to know each other quite well— and without wasting any time.

A slight change in music was a reminder that the evening was moving on. Dinner would soon be served. "It's a pleasure meeting you, Beth. Welcome to Washington," Ross said as he returned her to her aunt. Reluctantly, he made his way to the speakers' table.

≥⭑

Jacobs walked to the front of the room, stepped onto the platform, and crossed over to the podium. He looked out over the ballroom full of friends and acquaintances, who hushed their voices, recognizing that he was about to speak. Pushing all other thoughts from his mind, he welcomed those who were attending to support Senator Clement R. Rossiter II and called on the Reverend Mr. Franklin to offer the invocation. Jacobs then suggested that all the guests enjoy their meal, for soon they would be called upon to part with their money.

The audience laughed, and Jacobs returned to his seat at the speakers' table, where he sat between Senator Rossiter's wife, Gayle, and Ross. While plates were being put in front of them, the conversation centered around the beautiful niece of Catherine McKelvey and their anticipation of meeting her after the formalities of the evening. When that subject was exhausted, they spoke of food, then gradually each person became rather lost in his or her own thoughts. Having sat through countless such events before, Jacobs had no doubt that the Rossiter men were mentally reviewing the speeches they soon would make.

Jacob Jacobs allowed his mind to wander. As it did, his eyes traveled across two tables and then stopped. They lingered on Catherine, still as beautiful as she had been when she was Beth's age. Tonight she wore an elegant gown of black and silver, less ostentatious than usual, but just as striking. Catherine McKelvey, without trying, attracted attention.

What was she up to? Why did she bring her niece to Washington? She could have taken the girl with her to the Caribbean. If she were thinking of giving up her column, she could have asked that the girl work as her assistant and train her. He would certainly give the girl every chance to prove herself worthy of a position with the paper. Catherine would know that. According to her niece's work record, she was more experienced than Catherine had been when she began working with the paper. Jacobs had taught Catherine everything he knew back then.

That was a sobering thought, and Jacobs mentally shook away any further consideration of what Catherine might be up to. Maybe she was trying to punish him for what had happened more than two decades ago. Maybe she was trying to remind him. She needn't have bothered. No matter how hard he tried, awareness of Catherine McKelvey was never far from his mind—or his heart.

Now that she had asked him to keep an eye on her niece, Jacobs felt a tremendous dread deep in his soul. He didn't know much about the young woman, but he could tell a lot about her from the expression on her face and in her eyes when she'd been confronted by Ross Rossiter. It caused the line of an old song to run across his mind: *How you gonna keep 'em down on the farm after they've seen Paree?*

Under other circumstances, he and the older Rossiters might welcome the attraction between this young couple. But after what he'd read in that report and having seen this young woman, Jacobs knew something was amiss.

Something was disturbingly amiss.

five

Beth held disdain for swearing, feeling it stupid and profane, but she couldn't prevent the phrase *holy mackerel* from crossing her mind when she learned that she'd be living in the same house as such a charismatic character as Ross Rossiter III. Strange, Aunt Catherine had neglected to tell her about this son of Senator Rossiter. Whatever could her aunt be thinking?

"Is it proper for us to live in the same house?" Beth murmured as the two women headed for their table when Mr. Jacobs had stepped to the microphone and asked the guests to please be seated for the invocation.

"My darling," Catherine replied. "If you are proper, then yes, it is proper."

Beth had to nod and agree with that. But she was also aware of the Lord's Prayer including the line "lead us not into temptation." Before she allowed her fantasies to carry her beyond this fairy-tale night, she forced herself to realize that Ross Rossiter was probably married or at least attached.

A shot of reality struck her. *Well, so am I,* she thought, *attached, that is.* She had a future with Bob, which meant there was no room for fantasizing about the likes of tall, dark, handsome, wealthy, important, oozing-with-charm, enigmatic, romance-storybook type men. She chalked her straying thoughts up to the way she and her girlfriends had swooned over a movie star during her college days.

Just then, a waiter placed a bowl of the first-course soup in front of her. "What's this?" Beth whispered to Aunt Catherine, while the senators, representatives, and their spouses engaged in conversation after the prayer.

Beth felt a moment of chagrin when Catherine exclaimed, loudly enough for the entire table to hear, "Mmmm, this consommé julienne is quite tasty."

"I was just about to ask what this is," said a senator's wife.

Catherine's look at Beth and her grin caused Beth to realize that her aunt had tried not to embarrass her and was letting her know she wasn't the only one at the table who couldn't identify a dish at a glance.

"Now, what kind of beef is this?" another of the women asked, when the soup bowls were replaced with plates of meat and vegetables, along with bowls of salad.

"Yankee pot roast, is it not?" Catherine asked the waiter as he made his rounds of the table.

"Yes, ma'am," answered the waiter, wearing a black bow tie, white shirt, and black slacks. "With Madeira sauce. Then you have potatoes au gratin, broccoli Polonaise, and chiffonade salad with a dressing of tarragon oil and vinegar."

"What's for dessert?" asked one of the senators, whose girth indicated he'd had a lot of experience eating that course.

The others laughed as his wife nudged him with her elbow. "Marsh, you've hardly finished your first course and already you're thinking about dessert."

His lips pouted. "I'm just trying to join the conversation."

The waiter set the last salad bowl on the table. "Dessert is lemon sherbet fraisette topped with strawberries."

"I'll take Jean's," said Marsh, "since she isn't too keen on desserts."

"He probably will," his wife acknowledged, her eyes winkling.

Beth smiled at the way the two glanced at each other, reminding her of the light bantering that often went on between her parents.

Then the senator pointed his fork at Beth. "Now, extra calories is not something you have to worry about, is it, Beth? You're a beautiful girl. Take after your aunt Catherine."

Then the spotlight was on Beth. The everyday kind of talk about the food made her realize these were just ordinary people too, concerned with everyday things, even if they were often involved in making decisions that could change the way the entire world viewed many subjects.

She conversed easily as they exchanged stories of their hometowns and soon learned that several individuals at the table had come from small towns, even from poor families. A couple indicated their closeness to the Lord and said their support of Senator Rossiter was because of their respect for his faithfulness to his basic religious beliefs.

"We expect Ross to follow in his dad's footsteps," said the businessman sitting across from her. Marsh added in agreement, "He has a brilliant future ahead of him."

That kind of talk simply increased Beth's faith in her government, which so many people seemed to think was full of those interested only in power and position. Senator Rossiter was a religious man? Then his son must be also.

What kind man is Ross Rossiter? flitted through her mind. All those accolades—and a Christian too? She could not prevent her glance toward his table and swallowed too big a bite when his eyes met hers. She hoped the dimness of the lighting would hide the color she felt creeping into her face. She hoped, too, that a sip of water she took, as she forced her eyes to her glass, would not spill, but help the large bite she'd just swallowed go down.

This is downright silly, she told herself. *If I'm giddy about a room full of senators, some celebrities, and wealthy businessmen, what on earth would I do if I met the president?* Well, no one was more important than another in the sight of God. She knew that. But she did admire people who were in positions to make life-changing decisions, and she couldn't help but be a little overwhelmed.

Trying to keep her thoughts in perspective, she leaned back slightly as the waiter took away her plate and set the dessert in front of her. "The food was delicious," she said when Aunt Catherine's attention turned to her.

"It should be good food, darling," her aunt retorted again loud enough for all to hear. "At one thousand dollars a plate!"

"Amen," said the bulky senator as they all laughed.

❧

While dessert dishes were being gathered and coffee served, the man Beth had been introduced to as Mr. Jacobs walked to the microphone and asked the guests to enjoy their coffee while he made a brief introduction of Ross III, who would then introduce his own dad.

"Who, incidentally, needs no introduction," added the amiable Jacobs. "You're all here because you're supporters of the senator. I can only surmise that Ross has political ambitions. Therefore, he can't resist an opportunity to make himself visible and to promote an agenda."

Beth laughed with the others, then better understood the audience's laughter when Aunt Catherine leaned near her and explained, "Everyone knows that Ross has political aspirations."

She liked the down-to-earth manner and good-natured humor of the man Jacobs, whose voice was deep and warm, putting the crowd into an even more congenial mood. Earlier, when Aunt Catherine had pointed him out as the editor in chief of the paper who would be her boss and protector of sorts, Beth was struck by Jacobs looking like just another polished politician or wealthy business-man. Seeing him in front of the gathering of Rossiter sup-porters, however, she thought him quite pleasant and good-natured.

She liked his looks. He had a strong, handsome face, surrounded by dark hair that held a sprinkling of gray. He appeared extremely fit for his age, which she estimated to be about his late fifties. She doubted that his dark, intelli-gent eyes missed much, if anything.

&

"Good evening," Ross said as soon as he bounded in front of the microphone.

Those two words and a toothy smile were all he needed to get applause. His dad's constituents would be hoping Ross would someday fill his dad's shoes.

But Ross wouldn't dwell on himself tonight. Jacobs had taught him that just a brief appearance is enough to keep you in the mind of your public. Jacobs had said, "You don't need to force yourself upon them, lest they take a step back and take another look. Focus on the other fellow, and that will give you more positive attention than you'd gain by trying to impress the voters with your excellent attributes."

"What are my attributes?" Ross asked back then, sev-eral years ago when Jacobs had become his mentor.

Jacobs had laughed. "You look good if you stand straight

and don't hang over the podium. You have an automatic following because your dad's a senator. The voters expect you to be like him. At the same time, they will point out any flaws or qualities that are not up to his standards."

"I don't think I could ever fill his shoes," Ross had said.

Jacobs hadn't given him any false hopes. "It won't be easy," he'd said. "But you're young, and you have time to learn."

Ross was trying to learn, but the more he saw of his dad, the more he realized what a long, long way he, himself, had to go. And as Jacobs often reminded him, whatever he did was not only a reflection on his future political career, but a reflection on his dad as well.

The applause ended, returning Ross's thoughts to his audience. "My dad needs no introduction. You all know the senator. You're his supporters. You know his record of more than two decades," Ross began, "so there's not much I can tell you about that. But let me tell you what he was doing over Christmas and all through January when most people were home with family sitting around a Christmas tree and taking the New Year's holiday to make plans for the upcoming year. My dad took me and my mom away from the comforts of home to Kosovo."

Ross felt the adrenaline flowing the moment he'd stepped up on stage. He'd had that feeling when he acted in school plays and then again during a couple of years in summer theater. He'd never planned to be an actor, however. All he'd done since he was eight years old and his dad became a senator was to follow in his dad's footsteps. Working with the newspaper and being aware of differing opinions, along with his dad's and Jacobs's mentoring and his studies in acting, journalism, and communications, were all a part of preparation for his future. When his dad decided to retire, Ross would be ready to step in.

He'd gone on the campaign trail with his dad after getting his master's in communications. During the last election, his dad had given him an active part in the campaign so that he'd become a household face and a household name. Already, he had a feel for an audience. He could sense if they were with him or against him as soon as he started speaking.

There was no need to evaluate this crowd. They'd all come because they were supporters of his dad, and he'd been told they would support him when the time came. He knew Washington, and he was known. All eyes focused on him now, and he loved the rush it gave him. He would say what the audience expected and wanted to hear.

But one pair of eyes fastened on him gave him a different and new feeling. She looked as if she'd never heard such words before. She looked as if his words were new, exciting, meaningful, and not just another political speech to tickle the ears of supporters there so that they would open up their pocketbooks.

He knew what to say to please the others. He had them in his pocket. Or rather, their money would be in his dad's pocket, so to speak. Their support would make his campaign possible and successful. All Ross had to say was what his dad's constituents wanted to hear. And after being senator for more than two decades, his dad knew what his constituents wanted.

Ross figured he knew everyone in the room—except the niece of Catherine McKelvey. The others were no particular challenge. He knew how to tickle their ears. She was the challenge. She was the audience he hadn't spoken to before.

She was the one he wanted to impress with his speech.

&

Beth knew many politicians had made terrible mistakes and some were downright crooked. But she prayed for them daily and never lost her faith in leaders. She believed the majority of them wanted the best for their country and the people. Ross Rossiter III, from the moment he began talking about his family and what they had done over the holidays, renewed that faith.

He and his family had spent the holidays in Kosovo, where people were traumatized after seeing their homes burned and having their loved ones murdered before their eyes. The Rossiters had joined with members of a religious organization who, even though their lives were in peril while they worked in the Balkans, had been determined to bring Christmas to children in that devastated area.

Ross spoke of killings and bombings and an orphanage without electricity, and yet he praised his dad for caring about what happened in all parts of the world and wanting to do something to make conditions better. Ross was praising his dad, but Beth was thinking that Ross was right alongside his dad. If the senator were to be admired and respected for his concern for the needy, then so should his son.

Tears smarted Beth's eyes when he spoke of tragedy; she felt joy when he spoke of the good being done by the religious organization and the politicians who used their influence to encourage the American government to take a firm stand against violence and terrorism wherever it might occur.

It wasn't election time yet, but Beth cast her own secret ballot for the candidate of her choice—C. Ross Rossiter

III, known by his friends as Ross.

She would be honored to be counted as one of his friends and supporters.

six

Jacobs was as practiced as a politician in keeping his emotions hidden. More practiced, in fact, for he had been mentor and advisor to the senator for more than two decades. He was aware of how something as seemingly trivial as a glance could speak volumes. It was his job to watch the body language of the senator and his son and advise them about bad habits they might be developing.

Folding their arms across their chests could send the message that others should keep their distance. They should never cough into their hand and then extend it to someone for a handshake. The quirk of an eyebrow could lose a vote. They should never try to fake knowledge about a subject because there would always be someone more knowledgeable in the audience. And a cardinal rule of the political business was to never anger the press.

These cautions were simple but important reminders. Then there were the issues of utmost magnitude that would change the lives of Americans, oppressed people, and even the entire world. Jacobs was smart enough to recognize that he didn't know everything, but his job was to be smart enough to know who did know everything on a given subject. Then he could gather those people together to advise the senator on decisions he was facing.

There was no pressure this night. Everyone in the audience had paid one thousand dollars a plate to raise money for the senator's campaign. They were friends and constituents, and

Jacobs knew where each stood both in relation to the senator and on important issues.

Only one person had him stymied. And it was not the young beauty from South Carolina. He could read Beth like an open book. He knew her background from having gone over the investigative report. He knew by the way she reacted to those around her that she was open, sweet, and friendly. He could tell by the way she related to Catherine that she was completely captivated by her aunt. He also knew by the way she looked at Ross that she found him fascinating. And he knew by the way she listened to the senator talk about the needs in America and around the world and how he was a world citizen responsible to God and humanity that her faith was deep.

No, she was not the one he wondered about.

It was Catherine.

Catherine McKelvey had been the beauty queen from her state and came to Washington to participate in the Miss Cherry Blossom Pageant. Jacobs worked for several years for his dad, who had owned a well-known news magazine. After the magazine had been bought by another company, he became associate editor of the *Washingtonian Times,* which gave him the opportunity to cover the pageant.

Being young and single at the time, Jacobs had welcomed the opportunity, although he'd thought beauty pageants a trivial thing for pretty girls who had nothing else going for them but looks. As soon as he'd interviewed the first girl at the competition, however, his attitude began to change. Before long, he realized the contestants' beauty was just one asset among many outstanding qualities that all these intelligent young women possessed.

He'd gotten an education during that pageant. Mainly in

human nature. He felt sure he must have looked at Catherine as much as Ross was now looking at Beth Simmons—with open, genuine admiration. Had Catherine been as impressed with him as this girl was moved by Ross while listening to him?

Hardly! That was the difference. This girl had never been further than the Atlantic Ocean on vacation, and those places she had visited were no more than a four- or five-hour drive from her home. She had gone to the Biltmore House and Gardens in the mountains of Asheville, North Carolina, one time with her parents.

No, he didn't need to look at Catherine's near look-alike to remember how the aunt had looked when she was in her twenties. He could see her now, competing up on the stage in that patriotic little outfit of shorts, tails, and a top hat, twirling a baton to beat the band. Then she'd lit the ends of the baton. When he'd interviewed her, it was as if she'd lit a fire inside him. He hadn't known how to quench it. At the time he hadn't wanted to.

Realizing he was staring at the table where Catherine and her niece sat, he straightened and quickly scanned the room. Others might be watching him and wondering why his attention wasn't on the speaker. No, they were all busy watching the senator. And Catherine certainly wouldn't return a glance or acknowledge he looked her way.

Jacobs, who usually had success discerning the motives of world leaders and politicians around him, couldn't for the life of himself figure out Catherine.

But the more he thought about the situation, the more he knew what action he had to take. His obligation, responsibility, and duty was to the political careers of the Rossiters.

Much to his regret, further investigation into Mary Elizabeth Simmons's background had become imperative.

Saturday came while Beth's head was still swimming with all the activity of the week. First, arriving in Washington, D.C. Then shopping, followed by a wonderful campaign fund-raising dinner for Senator Rossiter. The following day she and Aunt Catherine had gone to the newspaper office where Beth again saw Jacobs and was introduced to the newspaper staff. Most of the time, Beth would be working from an office at the Rossiter house, just as Aunt Catherine worked from her home. But it was important to know the people she'd be coordinating her work with. She met her aunt's assistant society editor as well as Pamela, who Beth learned was a secretary who opened and sorted the "Ask Auntie" mail.

Beth wondered if a secretary were an unnecessary luxury until Pamela pointed out the boxes containing stacks of letters.

"We get this much every day," Aunt Catherine said. "Without Pamela, I would be taking all day just to sort these into categories."

"You see," Pamela pointed out, "Catherine might get twenty-five letters asking about the proper way to set a table for a dinner party. One wants to know how many spoons, where the fork goes, is the water glass to be on the left or the right, do you need a bread plate, does the woman sit on the left or right of the man—all kinds of details."

"I get breathless just thinking about it," Beth said.

They all laughed.

"Yes, it could seem like an impossible task to answer

everything. But I can answer all twenty-five letters in one response," Catherine explained. "That's why the letters are separated into categories. That way, I can read through and see how many I can respond to in the column. Some need a personal reply, and I usually have Pamela handle that."

"It must take a lot of research," Beth said. "I would have to look up the answers to most of those twenty-five letters about how to set a table."

"Exactly," her aunt agreed with a nod. "That's why we have books here, and I have them in my apartment, on almost every subject. Very helpful in etiquette and entertaining are these little books by Ann Platz and Susan Wales."

Beth looked at the attractive books Aunt Catherine took from a shelf: *Social Graces* and *The Pleasure of Your Company*. Beth made a mental note to read those for her own knowledge. For all she knew, she might have to choose between three or four forks at the Rossiter house.

❧

The phone was ringing when the two women returned to the apartment at Capitol House, and Aunt Catherine rushed to it before the answering machine picked up.

"Jacobs said you may pop in at any time this afternoon," she announced as she replaced the telephone receiver.

Beth gave a mock gasp. "That dignified man said 'pop in'?"

Aunt Catherine grimaced slightly. "Actually, no. 'Pop in' is my expression." She glanced toward the ceiling, thoughtful. "His exact words were 'might arrive.' "

Beth laughed. "Now that sounds more like what I'd think Jacobs would say."

Her aunt turned serious. "You and Jacobs have really hit

it off, haven't you?"

"I felt an immediate camaraderie with him the night you introduced us, after Senator Rossiter's speech," Beth said. "He strikes me as extremely intelligent but warm and friendly too."

"He is that," the older woman agreed. "I would not entrust you to him were he not. He is loyal to the Rossiters and to his work. And since his wife died five years ago, he is even more open about his faith in God. That should please you."

Beth nodded.

"Yes, well," Aunt Catherine said, "now we'd better get you packed. Jacobs will send Fred for your things whenever we call."

Beth looked at her aunt's back a moment. Only for an instant did she allow a reluctant thought to cross her mind. Aunt Catherine had always changed the subject when she or her parents talked about a deep faith in God.

After Beth had accepted the Lord Jesus into her heart at an early age, she'd been so happy to be a Christian that she had made a phone call to tell Aunt Catherine. "Are you a Christian?" she'd asked.

"Of course, darling. And I'm so pleased for you. Now, you have a birthday coming up. What would you like?"

Suddenly Beth realized that her aunt had always seemed to dodge any lengthy discussion about faith. Maybe she adhered to the adage that one shouldn't discuss religion or politics. But Beth liked the idea of discussing both. She hoped to do that with Jacobs and Ross.

Beth hadn't seen either man since the night of the campaign fund-raising dinner. How grand to be associated with a young man like Ross, just getting into politics. To be near someone actually involved in flag-waving, patriotism, inter-nationalism, decision-making, and action. She would be living in his house. She needed to please him, even more than Aunt Catherine and Jacobs. The paper she'd be writing for and the house she'd be living in belonged to the Rossiters.

Her pulse raced at the thought of going to the Rossiter house.

"Oh, don't rain on our parade," she wailed, parting the curtains across her aunt's sitting-room windows. Huge droplets splashed in disobedience against the panes.

Aunt Catherine laughed. "Just call it liquid sunshine."

"My hair curls when it's wet." Beth touched her hair like some glamorous star might do. "My, I'll make a terrible impression on the inhabitants of Rossiter house," she wailed, holding back a smile with difficulty.

Her aunt laughed at her theatrics. "Oh, my darling. You've made a wonderful first impression. Everyone thought you were adorable."

"That's because they say I look a lot like you, Aunt Catherine. On my own up here, I wouldn't even be noticed."

"But you are lovely. And you are my niece. And we're going to make the most of that—come rain or come shine." Aunt Catherine gave a determined nod. Now that was the aunt Beth knew—a woman who would not be daunted, come hail or high water.

After lunch, the rain had stopped, leaving behind a clearing sky. Aunt Catherine called, and Fred soon arrived to get Beth's belongings. The white-haired man in his seventies had no problem carrying the heavy bags and lifting them into the trunk of the long black car. Beth and her aunt hung garment bags on the rod behind the driver's seat.

"We'll take a cab," Aunt Catherine said, observing the

car full of Beth's old clothes, new clothes, and some of her own wraps and accessories. "No need for you to make another trip, Fred."

Beth followed her down the stairs and out the door and watched as her aunt rushed to the edge of the sidewalk, held her arms high, waving them like an eagle in flight, causing a cab to magically appear.

As soon as they were inside the cab, Aunt Catherine explained, "The Rossiter house is only a few blocks away, but those few blocks would bring you in contact with all the unsavory characters you'd ever hope not to meet. I don't want to expose you to the seamy side of life."

They both laughed. This was the kind of wild, fun sort of thing Beth expected of her aunt. Catherine McKelvey made everything seem like an adventure.

seven

"You know, I'd never ridden in a cab before I came to Washington," Beth said as their driver followed the car Fred was driving.

"Most of the time, taking a cab is the easiest way to get around in Washington. And you don't have to worry about parking."

Beth wasn't a natural worrier, but she couldn't help but be concerned about the impression she was about to make on Jacobs and Ross. Everyone at the campaign fund-raising dinner had been dressed to the hilt and smiling. It was a gala occasion. But now she would be going into the house where she would live for two months. Jacobs and Ross would see her day in and day out, not just in a working relationship but also after hours.

In journalism classes, Beth had learned that the first sentence of an article had to make a great impression. Then a writer had to hold the reader's attention with the second and the third sentences. How was she ever going to hold the attention of the Washington elite?

She hadn't time to worry about it too much, however. The cab pulled to the curb and came to a stop behind the black car that Fred had just parked and was unloading.

"We're only a few blocks from the White House," Catherine said, after paying the driver. "And like the other homes on the street, the Rossiters' was at one time a show-place. Many of the homes here are now business offices.

Some are apartments."

The house rose three stories with a round turret on each side of the front entrance, topped with great round copper domes that came together at the top like inverted ice cream cones. The white brick structure was only about ten feet from the sidewalk. In front of the turrets were bushes, brown and barren. Two cherry trees with tiny green pods closed up like folded umbrellas stood in the center of the small patch of yard on each side of the brick walk. Beth thought the house reminiscent of a fairy-tale castle she had seen pictured years ago in a storybook.

Then the prince appeared—Ross, dressed in blue jeans and a cream-colored knit shirt. Had he been watching for them? Her mind promptly answered the unspoken question with a firm *no*. He had come out to help Fred.

That potent smile of his, revealing perfect white teeth, seemed especially for her as Ross said with meaning, "Welcome, Beth, to Rossiter House."

"Thank you," she said to her host, walking past him as he headed for the car and her bags.

All week, she'd been treated like one of the Washington set. She'd met everybody but the president himself, and she wouldn't be at all surprised if the charismatic Ross Rossiter would someday be exactly that.

Now, glancing back at him taking a heavy bag from Fred's hands, she saw the cab drive away. Suddenly it was as if her coach had turned into a pumpkin and the horses had run away as mice.

She was not Cinderella at the ball. She was Beth from Podunk, USA, and an employee, like Fred.

Beth straightened, brushed her hair away from her face, took a deep breath, and braced herself for whatever lay on the other side of those double doors.

Her attention turned to the small foyer in which she stood, realizing the first doors, now open, were barred. The doors ahead of her were also barred, but they opened and the friendly face of Jacobs greeted her. Beyond him, in a spacious foyer at the bottom of a curving staircase reaching as high up as her glance took her eyes, stood a small, gray-haired woman in an everyday dress.

"Beth," Jacobs said, after greeting her aunt, "this is Mrs. Fred Nowens, the Rossiter housekeeper for many years."

"Nice to meet you, Mrs. Nowens," Beth said, shaking the woman's outstretched hand.

"Everyone around here calls me Trudy," the woman answered, smiling. "May I show you to your rooms?"

Beth quickly glanced at Aunt Catherine, who nodded, and Beth said, "Yes, thank you."

For the first time she had some anxious thoughts about her adventure in Washington. Aunt Catherine was a friend of the Rossiter family, particularly of Gayle, the senator's wife.

Beth was not a friend. Nor a guest. She was only an employee. She followed Trudy up the staircase with trepidation. In some books she'd read, employees of wealthy people were often housed on a basement floor. Others were housed on the top floor.

After having spent almost a week in Aunt Catherine's luxury apartment, would she now be relegated to the servants' quarters?

Beth held her breath as Trudy opened a solid mahogany door and gestured to Beth to enter. When she walked into the room, Beth couldn't believe her eyes. This was no servant's quarters. She had been transported to an earlier age.

Victorian wallpaper depicting a panoramic English country scene covered the walls above the mahogany wainscoting, and her feet sunk into a burgundy area rug that covered the beautifully restored wood floor. A small, electrified chandelier lit the luxurious sitting room that featured a Queen Anne writing desk and chair, two upholstered wing chairs on either side of a small fireplace, a couch, and an armoire that Beth suspected hid a television, VCR, and CD player from view.

Another door opened into the bedroom, which was located in one of the front turrets. Completing the suite of rooms were a tiled bathroom and large wardrobe. As Beth stood by the four-postered bed and gazed out over the busy street, she felt like a princess or Rapunzel. She gave herself a mental shake. The accommodations might be luxurious, but she was here to do a job, and she couldn't afford to lose sight of that fact.

❧

Jacobs had never known Ross to take such interest in his own home. He'd insisted upon showing Beth the house while they waited for dinner. All afternoon he'd behaved like a kid on a sugar high, and more than once his eyes had wandered up to Beth's suite on the second floor, where he had helped Fred deposit her bags in the hallway outside her sitting room door.

After Catherine left, Jacobs had asked Ross, "Are you going out this evening?"

"Nooo waaay," came Ross's firm reply. A short laugh escaped his throat as if Jacobs had asked an asinine question. Jacobs was not surprised. Ross apparently thought he'd found a new toy.

Jacobs went up into his own guest suite across the hall

from Beth after Trudy had taken up a glass of iced tea and a couple of Greta's famous chocolate chip cookies. He knew Trudy would have told Beth that she was welcome to roam the house. She would have offered to unpack for Beth, but Jacobs felt certain that Beth would not allow herself to be waited on. Then Trudy would have offered a snack and suggested that she might want to rest after an afternoon of unpacking and putting things away. She would have told her what time dinner would be served.

Apparently, Beth was taking Trudy's suggestion of the snack and rest. Ross finally accepted that fact and went to his own suite on the first floor. He'd commented that he would be sorting out some of his grandfather's notes.

But it was the comments of Catherine that caused Jacobs's concern. He sat in his swivel recliner and looked out at the rain clouds rolling in as they had earlier in the day. With his elbow on the chair arm, he rested his lips against his fist and index finger, a position that helped him think.

Catherine was someone he tried not to think about, but her parting words, after having said a reluctant good-bye to her niece, were, "I've deposited my niece, Jacobs. I expect interest on my investment, not a loss."

She hadn't laughed, nor even smiled, at that comment, so neither did he. Without waiting for a response, she turned to Ross and gave him an affectionate hug, said her good-byes to him, and then said she'd see them all in two months. "You know the saying, 'Don't call me.' Unless it's an emergency, of course," she'd quickly added.

Jacobs had stood silently as Ross continued to tell her to have a good trip and not worry about a thing, and to tell her traveling companion, Tippie St. Johns, the same. He would take good care of Beth.

Jacobs did not want to disillusion Catherine. But what was her mind-set on this? The awful thing was, he couldn't ask. He had no right to ask Catherine. . .anything. They both knew that. Quite well. And he owed her something. A lot. Anything she asked, he would attempt to do.

He could teach Beth something about politics.

He could teach her a lot about journalism.

But personal relationships? How was a man nearing sixty, without children of his own, supposed to chaperone a vital girl excited about politicians, while she lived in the house with Ross, an up-and-coming politician still sowing his wild oats?

How could Jacobs persuade two grown young people to do as he said—and not as he had done—in his own self-serving younger days?

He had a strong feeling his prayer life was about to become even more important. But was God in the baby-sitting and chaperoning business?

After Jacobs had taken a short rest and dressed for dinner, he went down to the library to read and wait for the young people. Ross joined him first, in a dress shirt and slacks. Soon afterward, they both turned when a soft southern voice said, "Excuse me. Trudy said I'd find you two in here."

Jacobs understood the admiring look of Ross when Beth strolled into the room that she would be working in, next to the office at the front of the house. Jacobs himself did a double take, instantly being plummeted into the past when he'd first seen Catherine.

Forcing himself to remember to forget the past, Jacobs greeted Beth warmly and asked if she would like to look over the contract and sign it. He watched Ross as he continued to look at her with a smile on his face, admiring the beautiful young woman dressed in soft, cream-colored trousers and a knit sweater of plum-colored horizontal stripes against a cream background. She unconsciously tucked a strand of hair behind her ear as she read, exposing a small gold earring. She crossed her legs, and a foot, wearing a plum-colored sling, began to swing back and forth. Jacobs had to smile, spying her plum-colored toenails.

Did she always smile?

About then, she looked up, met Ross's eyes for a moment, then shifted her gaze to Jacobs. "A pen, please. Before you change your minds about treating me so generously."

Ross took a pen from the desk and handed it to her. "I'm sure you're worth every offer in that contract."

"Don't you want to see a sample of my writing, or how I would handle the 'Ask Auntie' column?"

"That's Jacobs's department," Ross said.

Jacobs took it from there, after wondering briefly if he should mention an investigation. He decided to go with it. "Although I'm aware that Catherine wouldn't turn her column over to an incompetent, we do check out our employees. I know something about your writing background. In fact, I took the liberty of acquiring some of your articles from your hometown paper. I am impressed with your ability, Beth. You're a good reporter, and judging from your educational background and your religious faith, I don't think we have anything to worry about."

"You investigated me?" she asked playfully, her eyes sparkling. "That makes me feel so important."

Jacobs smiled. "It's just a matter of routine. It wouldn't be good for Ross's reputation if we were to someday discover he had a former flag-burner in this house. Or that someone lived here, even for a short period of time, who had not been cleared."

"I understand," she said, apparently unconcerned about an investigation. He wondered if she knew about the item in the report he'd received. Now would be the time to mention it. Did she know?

If she did, it apparently didn't make any difference.

Then. . .why should it make a difference to him?

He almost wished he hadn't asked for additional information. That should arrive any day now.

He glanced up as Ross's words penetrated his consciousness. The young man was taking the pen from Beth and returning it to a holder on the desk as he offered, "I'd love to show you the house."

"Thanks, I'd like that," Beth responded.

With his fingers resting gently against the small of her back, Ross led Beth from the room, leaving Jacobs looking after them in his contemplative mood.

❧

Upon entering the living room, Beth once again felt as if she were walking into the Victorian era. Her first impression was of an extremely long, deep-rose couch along one side of a white marble fireplace. Above the mantel stood a great gilded mirror, intricately carved and topped by two cherubs. To the right of the fireplace, an entire wall of windows matched those in the turret.

A quick perusal revealed soft pastel tones contrasted with deep, rich colors. There were elegant chairs in rose, blue, and antique white. Along a far wall stood a baby grand piano.

"Do you play?" she asked, lifting her face toward his.

"Not the piano," he said, mischief in his deep blue eyes that held her gaze for a long moment. "What about you?"

"I play a little," she said, "and sing okay with a group."

His eyebrows lifted slightly. "I do play a mean trumpet."

"Oh?" Beth found that interesting.

"Nothing professional. When I was in my early teens, a bunch of us got together and formed a band of sorts. I can still hear the squeaking and screeching as we played our favorite, 'It's a Grand Ol' Flag.' My granddad pretended it was the sweetest music on earth. I really miss that man."

Beth nodded. "Grandparents are special. I lost my mom's parents when I was quite young and my dad's just a couple years ago."

They moved across the room and into the inside of the round turret where five small-paned windows reached from the ceiling to the floor. Each was covered with sheer paneled curtains. Gold drapes hung at the sides, tied back with gold ropes.

Beth reached out to touch the marble statue of a woman in flowing Greek robes, a bow and arrows resting at her feet. "Now who might this be?"

"Diana," Ross said. "The Greek goddess of the moon and the hunt."

"She's beautiful."

"Yes," Ross agreed. "But I prefer flesh and blood."

Beth smiled and glanced down at the round rug beneath the statue, matching the carpet on the floor of the long, wide room. The carpet was a blend of all the colors in the room and fringed on the edges.

Ross's outstretched hand indicated they might go into the dining room, next to the living room. Beth stopped and turned toward him. "Thank you for inviting me to stay here."

"My pleasure," he returned.

eight

Beth was not surprised at the grandeur of the house, nor at the hospitable way Jacobs and Ross treated her. She knew they'd be cordial, but they were making her feel like she was a part of their family. She wanted to know them, and they seemed to want to know her.

Ross sat at the head of the table that could seat twelve people. She was glad they didn't sit at opposite ends. She was on Ross's right, and Jacobs sat across from her. Jacobs said grace, and Trudy served a delicious salad of strawberries and spinach with a touch of purple onion, feta cheese, and walnuts.

Between mouthfuls, the talk never lagged.

"What was the circulation of your hometown paper?" Ross asked.

"Twenty thousand," Beth replied, lifting her hand to bring her thumb and forefinger an inch apart, indicating it was small.

Ross shrugged, wearing a smile. "The quality of a columnist doesn't depend upon a paper's circulation but upon the skill of the writer."

"She has that," Jacobs added. "I'm sure she'll do fine."

"Oh, I'm sure," Ross added quickly. "I was just making conversation. Could I ask you a personal question?"

"Ask away," she said, sticking her salad with her fork, wanting another delicious bite before having to answer.

"Why would you leave a perfectly good job and come

here for a temporary one?"

She chewed fast and finally swallowed. "For the experience," she replied. "And I've always wanted to come to Washington. I think it's the most exciting city in the world." She knew her voice was rather breathless and her eyes would be shining.

"Just how many cities have you lived in, Beth?" Jacobs asked, and seeing a slight grin about his lips, she suspected he knew she'd lived in Henderson all her life.

"I can count them on one finger," she said, and they laughed. "But we've taken annual vacations in Miami, where my grandparents used to live. I have friends who've shown me pictures of their vacations in Europe and Hawaii. No matter what I was shown, I've always thought of Washington as the most exciting place. Maybe that's because of Aunt Catherine's influence."

She shrugged. "Anyway," she added, feeling suddenly guilty because she hadn't thought of Bob all day, "I thought now was the perfect time, while I'm waiting."

"Waiting?" Ross queried.

She nodded, as Trudy took away the salad bowls. "Well, not really waiting. My boyfriend is tied up with school. We wouldn't see much of each other until summer vacation anyway."

"Boyfriend?" Ross questioned. "You don't mind leaving him for two months?"

She really didn't. They would spend a lifetime together. She felt a twinge of guilt, wondering if her coming to Washington seemed like a frivolous fantasy of some kind to Ross and Jacobs. This was home to them, but it was almost heaven to her. She glanced from one to the other. "It's only three hours away by plane. We don't have to be apart the entire two months. Anyway, we're much nearer now than when Bob was getting his teaching degree in another state."

"He's a teacher, then," Ross said.

She nodded. "And a coach. He was a basketball star in college." She thought how juvenile that must sound. She might as well have added he was nice-looking. But she couldn't very well start expounding on Bob's qualities. He certainly had them. He had all the basic characteristics of a wonderful man and undoubtedly would be a good husband.

"Tell me something," Ross said, leaning back so Trudy could set a dish in front of him. "What's the difference between a boyfriend and a fiancé?"

That one was easy. Jacobs looked pensive, and Ross looked pleased with her response when she lifted her hand and wiggled her ringless fingers.

ร

Jacobs recalled that Catherine had mentioned that Beth was as good as engaged to a boy back home. Then why no ring? And if she planned to marry the boyfriend back home, why hadn't she said as much to Ross?

As if I didn't have a clue, he added to himself.

"This looks wonderful, Trudy," Beth exclaimed when the woman placed before them a platter of tomatoes stuffed with carrots and peas.

"I'll tell Greta," Thelma said with a meaningful look and grinned. "The cook always likes to hear compliments. And this," she said, taking a dish from the roll-in cart, "is flounder casserole."

They all helped themselves to the casserole.

"Croissants?" Jacobs asked, holding out the bread tray.

Beth and Ross helped themselves and then Jacobs put one on his plate.

He breathed a little more easily when the conversation turned to Kosovo. Beth said she was impressed with Ross and his father's involvement in the needs of that country. She spoke of a representative of an organization coming to her church, seeking funds to help war-ravaged countries, including Kosovo.

"It's the need that my family is most involved with," Ross said.

Beth nodded. "I was impressed with your dad's statement of faith in God." Jacobs glanced at Ross as Beth expressed her sense of awe about government. "I have a lot to learn," she said, "but I'm so interested in politics. This is the place where life-changing decisions are made. The president of the United States is the most powerful, influential man in the entire world. That is," she added, "when you judge by the world's standards."

Jacobs felt he knew exactly what she meant but thought it would be good for Ross to hear it from the young woman herself. "Clarify that, if you will, Beth," he urged.

"What I mean," she began, "is that power and prestige go a long way. But in the eyes of God, a person who proclaims His message of salvation is greater. God's message through that person determines the path leaders take and the decisions they make."

"You're absolutely right," Jacobs concurred. "Our nation is fortunate to have a president who is also a professing Christian and truly concerned about the welfare of this nation and the world. When a president of the most powerful nation in the world takes that kind of stand, then so do other leaders who influence the general public."

Ross laughed good-naturedly. "Jacobs never misses an opportunity to quote that verse from Proverbs. He even gave my dad a plaque with the inscription. Let's see, I think it says, 'When a country is rebellious, it has many rulers, but a man of understanding and knowledge. . .'" Ross glanced at Jacobs as if he might have forgotten all the words.

"Maintains order," the two men repeated together.

Ross laughed. "Each birthday and Christmas, I keep expecting a framed picture or a paperweight or something with that verse on it."

Jacobs snorted. "Really, Ross. Should a man your age be expecting a present from me at all?"

"Come to think of it," Ross said as if serious, "you are kind of stingy."

Jacobs deliberately gave Ross such a look of incredulity that Ross and Beth burst into laughter. "Seriously, though," Jacobs said, addressing Beth, "my wife and I had no children. Ross is like a son to me. I'm proud to be his mentor and friend."

❧

Beth liked the obvious affection between Ross and Jacobs. She felt honored that they included her in their circle of friendship. But that's because they were Christians, she was sure. A shared relationship with God formed a bond between people.

"I want to visit the churches in the area," she said, after swallowing a bite of buttered croissant. "Which one do you attend?"

"The church I attend—" Jacobs began.

"Jacobs!" Ross interrupted. "Why don't we take her with us to church in the morning? Instead of our telling her about it, she can see firsthand." He cleared his throat, and his eyebrows lifted. "You know. . ." he said, deliberately letting his voice trail away. Beth couldn't imagine why he grinned so, as if he knew a secret.

Jacobs was nodding. "Fine idea. And I think you're right. I suspect Beth will find this church interesting."

While Beth looked from one to the other, Ross asked, "Should we keep her in suspense?"

Jacobs put his fist to his mouth with his index finger against his lips, a gesture Beth had begun to realize was a trait of his. "Judging from her excitement about Washington and politicians, I daresay she needs to be forewarned. She might otherwise cause such a commotion, the church service would have to cancelled."

"Oh, I wouldn't do such a thing," Beth protested, laughing, so glad she wasn't going to be living with stuffy people but with those who openly liked each other and joked with her.

"Not even if you'll be in church with the two most powerful men in the world?" Jacobs asked.

Beth looked from him to Ross and back again. Realizing her mouth was open and she was staring from one to the other, she demanded, "What?"

"You see, the president always goes to church on Sunday when he's in town."

"And he's in town?" She was unable to keep the squeak out of her voice.

"See?" Jacobs shot a look at Ross. "Didn't I tell you? We can't take her there. She'll cause a riot."

Beth cleared her throat and made her voice low and serious. "The president's in town?" she asked, trying to sound as calm as if she were asking, "Are those madeleines that

Trudy has brought in for dessert?"

"In town, and he attends the same church Jacobs and I attend."

"You're kidding!"

"No," Ross said. "Well, I usually go to the worship service only, but Jacobs is in the same Sunday school class as the president."

Jacobs laughed and asked, "Would you like to go to Sunday school with the president of the United States—the second most powerful man in the world—and with the first most powerful, who will deliver a sermon to him?"

Beth could almost see the green sparkles that would be in her eyes as she exclaimed, "Oh, would I!"

nine

Uniformed guards stood outside the church, and men pretending to read newspapers sat in parked cars lining Sixteenth Street, where the church was located. Beth could hardly believe this was real, walking the few blocks from Rossiter House on Fourteenth Street to the church on Sixteenth and listening to Ross and Jacobs trying to outtalk each other for her benefit.

She learned the church was built in 1802, the sanctuary was shaped like a cross, and its most outstanding feature was the Redemption Window.

"There's a booklet about it," Ross said. "We can pick up one of those from a front table."

Beth felt so happy she could cry, but she knew better than to do that. It wouldn't do to open her purse and pull out anything, lest she be questioned by the not-so-Secret Service personnel.

As they neared the magnificent gray stone structure, Jacobs explained, "At 7:30 this morning, dogs would have sniffed out the church. For security, the Secret Service checks out closets, manholes, and even hymnbooks for bombs."

Beth felt the light pressure of Ross's hand at her elbow, as he nodded toward the right side of the foyer after they entered beneath a great arch, at which she felt reasonably sure were metal detectors. She didn't think all the men in dark suits whose hands were folded in front of them were deacons, either. Their sharp eyes darted from one parishioner to another, up and down, over and around. Secret Service—they had to be!

When Beth and her two companions reached the top of the narrow staircase, she saw that they were in the balcony. She could look down upon the sanctuary, empty and elegant, with a long, red-carpeted aisle between highbacked pews. A communion table, covered with a gold cloth and with a cross as a centerpiece, spoke meaningfully in its prominent place between two podiums. Behind the table hung a long red carpet, bordered in gold. Above it was a round, stained-glass window.

Ross's warm breath against her ear returned her to the present. "Let's sit at the back," he said in a low whisper. "That way you can see everything that's going on. Here, let me go in first. Jacobs can sit on the other side of you and explain some things. This is his Sunday school class."

Only two men were in the balcony when she, Ross, and Jacobs arrived. One immediately walked up to them. Jacobs introduced him as Mr. Phillips, the Sunday school teacher who had been a member of the church for fortyfive years.

"So glad to have you with us," Mr. Phillips said, his smile reaching his clear blue eyes, behind wire-rimmed glasses.

Jacobs leaned near. "You see the lectern in the center of the balcony, near the ledge?" When she nodded, he added, "That means Phillips is going to teach the class today. Sometimes the president teaches. Then the lectern is placed in front of one of those marble pillars. It's just another precaution since this space is open to the sanctuary below."

The balcony began to fill up from both sides. Ross leaned close to identify some dignitaries, noted visitors, and foreign ambassadors. When several dark-suited men came and stood in the doorway on the opposite side from where Beth sat, she could feel the tension in the room mount. All eyes seemed fixed on that doorway. Beth grasped the arm of her chair. Ross glanced at her, smiled, and placed his hand over hers.

When a trim, immaculate woman walked in, looking beautiful and fresh in a conservative, buff-colored spring suit, set off with a colorful silk scarf, Beth drew in a deep breath. Ross looked at her with a question in his eyes, and Beth nodded, indicating she knew that this was the First Lady.

"That's her mother behind her," Ross explained. Beth watched as the two women and the man—the president of the United States—spoke and smiled to others as they walked along the front of the balcony, searching for seats, which they found on the second row of the middle section.

A man, introducing himself as Will Moore, stood to welcome the guests, had them stand, tell who they were, and where they were from. Beth heard places like Washington, India, Brazil, and New York, as well as her own contribution of Henderson, South Carolina. Then Mr. Moore introduced the teacher, telling the class what Jacobs had told her about his being a member for a long time. "He was once asked what his objective was, being the president's teacher," Mr. Moore said. "Paul Phillips replied, 'My objective is to please God.' "

Several "Amens" sounded, and Beth thought one of them came from the president himself.

Mr. Phillips got up and said, "Let us pray."

Most of the prayer was like any she might hear in her own church, with one addition—asking God's blessings and guidance on the president and on the nation's political leaders.

After the prayer, Mr. Phillips said, "Today we're going to talk about marriage. Now, we know men and women were created in God's image. Then, is there a difference between a man and a woman's role in marriage?"

Wow! He sure could jump in where angels feared to tread, Beth was thinking. That was a debatable subject, and when she'd heard it discussed before, different sides backed up their arguments with Scripture. She was anxious to hear what these people of prominence had to say.

"Adam was a rough draft," said a well-dressed woman from the other side. "Then God created woman."

The group responded with light laughter, and so did Mr. Phillips.

A dignified-looking man said, "Man was a happening; woman was a creation."

"There's one thing for sure," Mr. Phillips said. "If a man has enough horse sense to treat his wife like a thoroughbred, she'll never be a nag."

After brief laugher, Mr. Phillips added, "Let's look at what God's Word has to say." He then called the First Lady by her first name and asked her to read the Scripture from the book of Ephesians, chapter 5, verses 22–33.

Beth thought it impressive that the first lady stood while she read from the Word of God. Afterward, she and the first family blended in with the others and were not given any preferential treatment. There was even disagreement about some points.

But the highlight of the discussion occurred when Mr.

Phillips asked, "Mr. President, do you remember the answer you gave to the question about the Bible last Sunday?"

The president became a mere human being as he slowly shook his head. Good-natured chuckles sounded as Mr. Phillips admitted, "Neither do I, but I know it was a good point."

The president, however, redeemed himself later by his knowledgeable answers and discussion of the lesson.

When the lesson was finished, Mr. Phillips asked the members to please remain seated after the closing prayer. The president, the first lady, and her mother left the class when Secret Service agents appeared at the doorway.

Beth accepted a church bulletin from an usher as they filed into the sanctuary. Ross walked over to a table and brought her a booklet about the church. At a certain point, a sign read, "Church members only beyond this point."

"Let's sit back here today," Jacobs said, before they reached the sign. Beth saw the president and his family sitting four rows from the front. Guards stood along the outer aisles during the service. Beth opened the booklet and read about the Redemption Window.

It was a five-lancet window, and across the bottom was written, "Whosoever believes in Him shall not perish, but have everlasting life." The five scenes depicted people of the Bible. The focal point was an image of the redeeming Christ, crowned with a wreath of thorns, symbolizing His sacrifice of His life for the world's salvation.

A sense of God's presence permeated Beth as she read about the purpose of the Redemption Window, "created in the nation's capitol where the Lord might extend His invitation to thousands of people who pass by." She read about the colors, whose glory lay in the movement of light. The analogy was made of an orchestra, with ever-changing patterns of tones and hues.

Red represented love, valor, and martyrdom.

Blue meant wisdom, loyalty, truth, and heaven.

Yellow symbolized goodness and spirituality.

She read that the congregation wanted the kind of building that would be a ministry, a place that made it easy for people to find God and hard for them to forget Him.

Looking up with a smile on her face, she realized that goal had been reached.

Ross and Jacobs must feel it too, she thought, as they all stood to sing, "All Hail the Power of Jesus' Name," and the men on each side of her sang out in deep baritone voices fit for any choir.

After a meaningful sermon, titled "Born Again," the congregation sang, "Take My Life and Let It Be Consecrated, Lord, to Thee."

A notice in the church bulletin advised the congregation that in a service attended by the president of the United States, they should remain seated until the president had left the church and the organ postlude began. When it was time, the congregation sat in expectant silence. Several men and women rose from their seats, gathered around the presidential family, and left by a side door.

As Beth, Ross, and Jacobs walked out of the church into the cloudless spring day, Beth whispered a silent prayer of thanks to God and an appreciation for her aunt Catherine, who had given her in less than a week the most wonderful experiences of her entire life.

ten

After changing into comfortable shorts and a T-shirt, Beth propped up on her bed and called her parents. Hearing their voices reminded her of how dear they were to her. But she couldn't say she had missed them. She'd been too busy doing and seeing and going.

She told them all about going to church, then to the Capital Hilton Hotel's five-star restaurant for lunch. "Oh, I'll send you the article in today's paper. It's about Senator Rossiter's campaign fund-raising gala. That's on the front page. But. . .wait 'til you hear this. I'm on the society page, right along with Catherine and her important friends. Even my name was in the caption below the picture."

"And what is the senator like?" her mom asked.

Beth hesitated before telling them he was a fine Christian man, and she mentioned his involvement in Kosovo, which they found impressive. She knew they had the impression she was living in the senator's home and had no idea that a young, single C. Ross Rossiter III was staying there as well. She saw no reason to reveal something like that which might cause them any concern about gossip.

"Catherine bought me the most fabulous outfits," she said, changing the subject quickly.

Her mother laughed. "That's not surprising. She's always sent you lovely things. And she dresses so beautifully. I suppose she's in the Caribbean now."

"Yes, she called the day she arrived. But I haven't heard

from her since that day."

"Your mom and I are going down to Isle of Palms for a week," her dad said.

"That's great," Beth said, realizing they had never had a vacation without her since she was born. Even after she had grown up, she went along with them and sometimes took a girlfriend. Maybe it was part of growing up that made you begin to see your parents as having a life of their own.

After hearing their "Good-byes," "I love yous," and "Be carefuls," Beth called Bob. Normally on a lovely spring day, they'd be spending the afternoon at the swimming pool in her parents' backyard. He often ate lunch with them after church, and sometimes they went out. What would he be doing today?

When he answered, she asked him that very question.

"Grading papers," he said. "I gave a history test Friday."

"Anything exciting happening there? You know, all work and no play. . . ," she teased. Her mind filled in the rest— *makes Bob a dull boy*. Now why did she think such a thing? Of course, she knew. Just like the Isle of Palms couldn't compare with Washington, D.C., in her mind, neither could a history test compare with going to church with the president of the United States.

After a moment, she realized her mind had wandered while he was telling her about the ball game he'd played in Friday night and how that was why he had had to grade papers over the weekend.

"That's wonderful, Bob."

"Wonderful?" he quizzed. "Beth, I just said we lost."

"Oh, well, it was a good game, though."

"Not really," he returned shortly. "The score was ten to zero."

"Oh," she said, remembering she had heard him say ten to zero. "I thought your team made the ten."

"Beth, it's obvious you're not interested in our little games here. Go ahead and tell me what's on your mind."

She felt guilty. Her spirits were dampened. However, she told him there was a Ross III, who along with Jacobs made her feel like a member of their family. She told about going to church and sitting in the class with the president.

"President of what?" he asked.

"The United States," she blurted, chagrined.

"I knew that, Beth. I was just trying to be funny."

"Oh," she said, and tried to laugh. It wasn't funny. "You're not impressed."

"I'm impressed with you, Beth. I miss you."

"I miss you, too," she could honestly say. Of course she missed people who were close to her. But she couldn't say she wished he were there. Could she say she wished he were in Washington? Did she really want Bob to be there, have a light supper with Ross, and then the three of them watch TV?

She should not feel guilty that her answer was no. This was her adventure—not Bob's.

"I'll be home before you know it. Or you could come up here."

"Now there's an idea," he said. "Some weekend. Are the cherry blossoms out?"

"Working on it," she replied.

"I'll give it some thought—about coming up there," he said.

His saying he might come to Washington disturbed her. The cost of plane fare would make a sizeable down payment on an engagement ring. Or, if he were extremely economical, it would even pay for a small diamond, wouldn't it?

She couldn't tell him that, however. "Great," she said. "Just let me know. There are plenty of bedrooms here in Rossiter House."

"I love you, Beth."

"I love you, too."

After hanging up, she thought about Bob. They would have a lifetime together.

But strangely, the elation she was feeling was not initiated by her talking with Bob. And the picture in her mind was not of sitting by the pool or watching Bob grade papers. Rather, it was the feel of the soft fabric of Ross's suit against her arm—the warmth of his hand when it had covered hers, the depth of his gaze just before the opening prayer in the Sunday school class.

Something in her wanted to be in step with him, to feel his smile, to be lost in the depths of his gaze. Perhaps she should have dinner in her suite, then write down her private thoughts in her personal journal.

All part of the fairy tale, she told herself. *Perhaps.* But, she would at least join Ross and Jacobs for dinner. She didn't want to lose this "happily ever after" feeling just yet.

੨

"I didn't know you were into quiet Sunday evenings reading or watching TV," Jacobs said to Ross after dinner as they watched Beth disappear into her rooms off the second-floor hallway.

Ross turned from where he'd been watching the beautiful woman, thinking how delightful she was in so many ways. He grinned and spread his hands. "People change."

Jacobs gave a quick nod. "You might remember that, in this instance, I'm responsible for what happens to this girl."

"Woman, Jacobs," Ross reminded him, while removing his suit coat and loosening his tie. "A twenty-five-year-old woman with a mind of her own."

"We all have a mind of our own, Ross. But yours is thirty-two and hers is twenty-five. That makes my mind more mature than the two of yours put together. And I'm saying to you that this girl needs to leave here after two months, not with a broken heart, but with the kind of memories she can cherish for a lifetime."

"I quite agree," Ross said, and chuckled before tossing his coat over one shoulder and striding off to his rooms. When he glanced back, Jacobs wasn't even smiling. He still stood beneath the stairs, wearing that pensive, warning look in his eyes.

Ah, well. He couldn't stand there forever.

Back in his room, Ross tossed his coat across a chair, and his tie soon followed. As he changed into more comfortable clothes, suitable for a quiet evening at home, he smiled.

He found it refreshing to see someone excited about Washington and politics, instead of filled with disdain and disillusionment. It renewed his enthusiasm for politics and reminded him that voters wanted to have faith in their government. His dad had done a lot of good over the years and passed many bills that were helpful to the public. Scandal hadn't touched his dad.

"You're following in his footsteps," Beth had said during dinner.

"Well, at times I have to try and dodge the press. Unless Dad runs for president, I can pretty much do as I please, in private, that is."

Jacobs had frowned. Beth had smiled. Ross wondered if

she had an inkling of what he wanted to do in private.

Ross knew Beth was not accustomed to the fast pace of Washington nor to the fast pace of life. That enhanced her appeal. The women his age were single for some good reasons—or putting a career first, like Catherine McKelvey said she had done when she turned down her numerous admirers when their attentions went beyond friendship.

Other women his age were divorced or married. Not that he didn't understand that some were divorced for very good reasons. Yet the fact remained, part of Beth's appeal was that freshness about her—a certain purity and innocence. That appealed to him.

After his breakup with Carlotta, the Italian ambassador's daughter, he'd suspected he would never find another girl who inspired him to that extent. He hadn't expected to find one in Kosovo, there wasn't an available one in the campaign headquarters that appealed to him, and he'd already dated and dropped all the other young women he knew.

He'd heard his dad say that when you help others, it comes back to you, even though you don't serve for personal reward. Well, he'd gone to Kosovo because his dad had asked him. Now, look what had happened. And it wasn't even his birthday.

But there she was—a pretty unspoiled present on his doorstep, so to speak. Ah, better than that. She was upstairs in a bedroom that belonged to him.

He thought that kissing her would be like eating ice cream for the first time—all sweet but never satisfying enough. You always wanted to go back and have another scoop. He did not like the idea of even her boyfriend having kissed those lips. He didn't know any girls who adhered to the adage he'd heard somewhere, about not kissing on a first date. It was probably small-town morality, and Beth most likely adhered to it. Wasn't today a first date of sorts? They hadn't kissed, and that brought to mind another adage: Absence makes the heart grow fonder.

He just realized the adage worked in more ways than he had imagined. The absence of passionate kisses only enhanced his desire to make Beth his own.

How long should he wait? A week? Two?

eleven

When Beth went down to breakfast early Monday morning, Jacobs was sitting at the booth in the breakfast nook. Ross stood at the island bar, choosing from an array of breakfast dishes, including cereal and fresh fruit. After she and Ross sat, Jacobs said, "Let's ask God to bless the food." He said the prayer while they bowed their heads and closed their eyes.

Whatever apprehension she might have felt just vanished. It was as she had supposed. Christians had a common bond, no matter whatever differences there might be in their lives. In no time at all, the three of them were chatting about everything from what her favorite foods were to what the paper said about the senator and the president.

The nicest thing happened after breakfast when Jacobs asked if she'd like to join him in his morning devotions. Ross said he needed to make a few calls and then get down to campaign headquarters. Beth had already had her devotions, but she was delighted that she and Jacobs could spend a few moments worshiping God and reading His Word. No wonder this man had become such a success. He had things in the right perspective.

After devotions, Beth and Jacobs went into the library where Jacobs instructed her on her computer, a kind she was familiar with, gave her the newspaper E-mail address and fax number, as well as a personal E-mail address.

"Your time is your own," he said, "as long as you get

the columns in on time. And if you need us, my secretary and I will be in the next room."

A woman's voice sounded from the doorway. "Did I hear my name?"

Jacobs turned, and a thin, short woman who looked to be around his age walked in. Her silvery white, boyish, bobbed hair moved softly at the sides of her face as she neared the desk so that Jacobs could introduce them.

"Mrs. Millicent Cooms," he said, "without whom we'd all be lost."

"Flattery will not replace my annual raise, Jacobs," the woman said firmly.

"I've found that out over the years," he returned, then smiled. Beth could see they liked each other.

"Oh, I have Beth's press card and expect to get confirmation today that she's included in the reception."

"Fine," Jacobs said. As Millicent returned to the office, Jacobs explained. "Since you're now under contract with the newspaper, you will be included in the annual local journalists' reception on Friday."

"Hmmm," she said with a lift of her eyebrows, "that sounds impressive."

"It usually is," he agreed. "It's held at the White House."

How am I supposed to work on Monday—with next Friday and the White House on my mind? Beth wondered a short while later, looking at the stack of letters dropped off by Pamela the previous Friday. After separating them into light and serious subjects, she decided to start with the light ones.

She laughed when she came upon one from "Desperate Phil."

Dear Auntie,

For eleven years my house dog, Chumley, has laid at my feet while I read the evening paper after coming home from work. Recently, I've been working late, and when I come home, he's in my chair. When I make him get out, he tucks his tail between his legs, drops his head, and honestly looks like he's crying. He gets at my feet but looks up at me with such an accusing expression, I feel guilty. Should I let him have my recliner?

Desperate,
Phil

Beth thought of replying, "What would you do if Chumley decided he wanted to drive your car?" But on second thought, although some subjects were lighter than others, if someone cared enough to write a letter about something, then she should treat each question as serious. She closed her eyes and asked God to help her answer in a way that would benefit the questioner, no matter how trivial the subject might seem to her.

Dear Desperate Phil,

I think your "dog daze" situation calls for "tough love." Apparently Chumley has become like a family member. But dogs, like children, are unable to make adult decisions, and we must use loving discipline in order to make their, and our, lives acceptable. A guest in your home might consider it rude for a dog to be treated with more dignity than you treat yourself. If you had a child and the child wanted to take over your favorite chair,

*would you allow that? Since you asked, you're
apparently in doubt. A good rule of thumb is, "If in
doubt, don't do it." When he jumps into your chair,
just demand, "Down, boy!"*

*Your dog has been your best friend for eleven years.
The change in him might be because your work
schedule has changed. Talk with Chumley's vet about
this situation during your next visit.*

*And, Phil, what a beautiful word picture you have
painted of his lying at your feet.*

Lovingly tough,
Auntie

Beth printed it out and took it in for Jacobs to read.

"Perfect," he said and applauded.

"You think Catherine would be pleased?"

"Catherine is so pleased with you already, I doubt anything would shake that confidence." He smiled. "Believe
me, you have not let her down."

Beth breathed deeply, then stood. "Could I get you a
cup of coffee or something?"

"Trudy could do that," he said.

"I know," she said, "but I would like to do something for
you. I know you're the editor in chief, with all the power
that goes with that. But you have made me feel so comfortable with you, like I'm just a coworker. I know we joke
around like I'm an equal with you and Ross. But. . .I know
who I am, and where I come from."

Seeing that pensive look come onto his face and notic-
ing how he broke their gaze, Beth wondered if she'd gushed
too much and embarrassed him. But he smiled gently. "I
take my coffee black, thank you."

Jacobs sat with his fingers against his lips. Did Beth really know as much about herself as she thought? He almost wished he hadn't put the investigators on a more extensive background check. Some things were best left alone.

But it was done. And the report could come through anytime now. Had he gone beyond investigating and begun snooping? And what if, by chance, the report did reveal more puzzling developments? How far should he go with his inquiries?

How far would Catherine want him to go?

Did Catherine really only want him to give this adorable girl a chance to have a little fun and gain experience in Washington? Could it possibly be so simple?

Was anything ever simple—with Catherine?

But he needed to stop thinking of Catherine, however difficult that was, with this young reminder before him daily. Seeing the happy girl at the doorway with their coffee and a cup for Millicent, he tried to focus on the matters at hand. This girl was bringing a lot of joy into this otherwise rather staid household.

By Thursday, Ross's suspicions he'd had that first night he saw Beth were verified. As he stood before his bathroom mirror and shaved he concurred—*she has everything!* She had beauty, brains, and moral character. Her appearance at home and in public was conservative and impeccable. Her freshness and enthusiasm drew people to her. And too, she gave every indication, without being flirtatious, that she liked him.

He liked that!

He watched his own smile widen, admitting that the

thought of her was more invigorating inside and out than the bracing tingle of the aftershave he splashed on his face and neck.

Catherine had probably instructed Beth well. Many times he'd heard Catherine say after a successful match-making scheme, "I like the old-fashioned way. A girl should chase a guy until he catches her." He liked the challenge presented by Beth's reserved way of pretending she wasn't pursuing him.

Well, if Catherine had in mind a matchmaking scheme, he would like to thank her. He seriously doubted that Beth dressed like a Washingtonian in Small Town, South Carolina. She'd been a knockout in her red suit on Sunday. He could hardly wait to see what she'd wear to the White House.

Soon he slipped on his suit coat, straightened his tie, ran his fingers along the side of his thick curly hair, and smiled at his reflection. Just that morning at breakfast he'd made the comment, "She'd be terrific working at Dad's campaign headquarters."

"She needs to get settled into her job, Ross. Let's not rush her," Jacobs had said with that steady gaze of his that spoke volumes that his lips didn't. With a glance, Jacobs revealed he knew what was in the back of Ross's mind, and he wasn't going to let him get away with it.

Well, we'll see.

She likes me. She liked my introduction of Dad that first night. She has obviously enjoyed my company. Rush? She's only going to be here for two months. Every good journalist knows an introduction is only the teaser. Let's get to the heart of the matter. Heart? No, on second thought, let's keep the heart out of it.

She was a smart girl. Instead of trying to please him, she went about her business, being her own person. That was admirable. Having morning devotions with Jacobs was a good move too. *She certainly had reeled him in. And, pretending to have a boyfriend too!*

Shaking his head, he chuckled. A young woman, serious about a man, wasn't going to leave him for two months in order to write an advice column. Oh, this was great! This was Catherine at her best!

Still smiling, he closed the door of his suite, bounded down the stairs, and with a spring in his step and a purpose in his stride, walked across the foyer. Sneaking glances to ensure neither Jacobs nor Beth were near, he went into the library. At Beth's desk, he took from his pocket the question he'd typed the day before and stuck it underneath the top question in the stack labeled "serious."

twelve

Friday finally arrived. When Ross strode into the foyer, he looked at Beth and exclaimed, "Fabulous!" Moments before Ross arrived, Jacobs had said she looked very beautiful.

Beth felt reassured. She'd been uncertain about how her wardrobe would fit in with the more formal attire that characterized the nation's capital. Now, thanks to Catherine's shopping expertise, she felt both beautiful and fabulous in the camel-colored skirt that fell to just above her knees and the camel and navy striped jacket with its gold-toned buttons down the front. A double row of four large buttons each gathering the sleeves into a pleat was the perfect touch to make the outfit sophisticated and, yes, fabulous. Catherine had picked out the navy and camel, linen and leather spectator pumps and large clip-on earrings matching the gold buttons.

Beth wanted to be dressed appropriately for the reception, and she prayed that she would do nothing unseemly to embarrass these important men with whom she was working.

Almost as soon as their car left Rossiter House, the threesome neared the White House. The immaculately trimmed lawn and hedges, lushly green, were an impressive sight. Patches of vivid red, yellow, and white were much in evidence, along with the pink buds about to open into full-blown cherry blossoms.

"What's that?" Beth asked, peering out the window.

Ross leaned over, his face so close to hers she could smell the faint scent of aftershave or cologne.

Across from them, Jacobs peered out and laughed at the sight of a turkey strolling freely across the White House lawn.

"There's a headline for you," Ross said. "Turkey on the White House Lawn."

Beth turned to find herself looking straight into Ross's dancing eyes. "Won't the readers think we're talking about the president?"

Jacobs chuckled. "Depends on whether you're a supporter or an opponent."

Ross smiled, and he didn't take his eyes from her. She found it rather difficult to look away from him and felt the warmth of a flush covering her face. She could still feel his presence, even after he sat back against the seat.

Soon, the limo turned and became one of a long line of cars slowly making their way along a curved drive to the side of the White House.

"Security will be tighter than usual," Jacobs said. "The king and queen of Belgium have been guests for several days, and there are rumors that something big is underfoot."

Beth couldn't help but smile at that thought, as a security officer opened the limo door and she stepped out onto White House ground, while a turkey strolled by as if it owned the place. The turkey was out of place, like her, but the turkey didn't seem to know it.

Security guards checked identification and matched their names with those on a list of authorized press personnel. After the three guests passed through a metal detector, guards stood aside and allowed them to ascend the stairs to the second floor, where in the main foyer, for their pleasure, stood uniformed band members playing violins.

"In case you don't recognize the uniforms," Jacobs said, when they had passed out of hearing range, "the four men are marines and the woman is an army officer."

Only muted whispers were heard as the group, now becoming a crowd, passed the musicians and were led to a room that Jacobs quietly identified as the State Dining Room.

Around two sides of the room, tables covered with white cloths were laden with cheeses of all descriptions, elegant thin crackers, and napkins with the White House Seal. The uniformed attendants behind the tables looked at name tags and addressed the guests by their first names as if they were old friends and frequent guests in this lovely home.

On second thought, Beth realized as she filled a small, gold-rimmed crystal plate with cheese and crackers, many of the guests were frequent visitors. Being the son of a senator, Ross had undoubtedly been here many times. And Jacobs obviously had, even knowing the names of each room.

"Beth," the congenial attendant said, "what would you like to drink?"

Quickly surveying her choices, Beth answered, "Orange juice, please." As he poured her choice into a long stemmed glass, she picked up two of the small square napkins—one for her lips and one for her purse.

"Thank you," she said, and smiled, reaching for the long-stemmed glass.

Beth recognized a few people she'd met at the newspaper office. Jacobs and Ross introduced her to several other reporters from competing local papers as they wandered at leisure while she admired cabinets filled with serving sets of past presidents and the china, gold, and silver from which they had eaten.

When Jacobs stopped to talk with his associate editor, Ross led Beth to paintings and sculptures of previous presidents and first ladies. It was a world of history, more real than anything she'd ever read in a textbook. She toured various colored rooms: red, blue, green.

"Is there a ladies room nearby?" she whispered to Jacobs when he caught up with them.

"Out into the hallway, turn right, and you'll find it on the left. It isn't labeled, but it will be the closed door. Labeled ones are on the first floor. Oh," he added, as she started to walk away, "hurry back. The photographers and security are gathering around the Diplomatic Reception Room. That indicates we may have the pleasure of a visit from someone quite noteworthy."

"Not the turkey?" Ross quipped.

Jacobs shrugged. "Again," he said, "depends."

They grinned at each other and Beth hurried away.

Almost immediately upon her return, the guests were being ushered into the Diplomatic Room. After the journalists and their employers were seated, the First Lady appeared from a side door and a small path was cleared for her. She stepped around planters of camellias that surrounded the dais and walked over to the lectern.

Beth thought her a first lady to be immensely proud of. As on Sunday, she was conservatively dressed in a lightweight suit. Poised, refined, and lovely, she looked around at her audience and welcomed them to her home. Her manner and attitude were warm and cordial.

"The president regrets that he cannot be here. He is in conference with the king of Belgium. But he asked me to read a statement to you." She read greetings, regrets, and appreciation to the press for their excellence in adhering to standards of high-quality journalism and presenting unbiased reporting.

Beth thought that if some were not unbiased, this speech might convict them or motivate them to hold to a higher standard. Of course, that would be the purpose of the speech, and the responsibility of a nation's leader included reminding those under his leadership how they should adhere to high moral standards.

The respectful standing and thunderous applause at the conclusion of the First Lady's comments indicated that everyone was satisfied with her gracious words of welcome. Then she stood in the hallway, shaking hands, greeting and speaking to each of the guests as if it were no imposition at all and she wanted them to feel perfectly at home.

"How are you Ross? Jacobs?" she asked when it was their turn. Beth did not think she called them by first names because of a name tag.

She was sure of it when Ross introduced her as Catherine McKelvey's niece, filling in for Catherine's column while she was in the Caribbean.

"Oh, I see the resemblance," the first lady commented. "I never miss reading Catherine's column," she said. "I'll look forward to yours. Please tell Catherine we miss her but hope she's having a wonderful time."

"I'm sure she is, but I'll be sure to tell her," Beth said. "It's so nice to meet you."

They quickly walked on, giving others a chance to be

greeted by their gracious hostess. Beth could hardly believe she had just stood face-to-face with the first lady, chatting away as if they were two ordinary persons.

I suppose we are, in a sense, she realized. Having seen the First Lady in Sunday school helped her keep things in perspective. In the ultimate sense, every individual was one of God's ordinary people—He just had different roles for them to play in life.

Back in the limo on the way to Rossiter House, Beth could not stop talking about how blessed she felt to have had such a privilege. She thanked them profusely. "And I even got a souvenir."

"What?" Ross blared. "I hope you didn't steal any silver or gold."

"Silver and gold have I none," she quipped, seeing his grin. She opened her purse and took out a small square napkin and laid it on her lap. Then she took out a larger, rectangular, cream-colored paper towel engraved with the same national gold seal that was on the napkin.

She waved it in front of them. "How many people can boast of an engraved paper towel from the White House potty?"

The two men laughed heartily. They probably thought she was some kind of kook—but Jacobs said, "You are truly a delight," and Ross was nodding as if he agreed.

Thank You, God, she said silently, as she did many times each day, *for the blessing of letting me come to Washington and be involved with such wonderful people.*

thirteen

Over the weekend, Ross hadn't had much time to think about the question he'd sneaked into Beth's office. He'd had a campaign meeting on Friday night and was at his dad's most of Saturday going over some of their strategy.

Beth had spent much of Saturday writing E-mail messages to Pamela, asking her to send personal notes to some of the questioners whose letters would not be answered in the column. He admired her conscientiousness and didn't attempt to suggest anything different when she mentioned at dinnertime that she was going to write in her journal and perhaps read for awhile.

They again attended Sunday school and church on Sunday, although the president and his family weren't there.

Monday morning, Ross tried not to show his eagerness to read her column. He'd appeared at the breakfast table earlier than usual in time to hear the ending of a story she and Jacobs had read from a book called *Chicken Soup for the Christian Soul.*

"Every one of these stories make the tears well up," she said, wiping her eyes with a napkin. "Jacobs and I read one after we read from the Bible."

"What I'm anxious to read this morning," Ross said, while dishing food onto his plate, "is what you've written in your column." Trying not to act overanxious, he took a bite of food, said, "Mmmm, good," and washed it down with orange juice. Then he picked up the paper and turned to her column.

A quick scan revealed his question had not been answered. He tried not to show disappointment by reading each question and answer carefully. He laughed at the "Desperate Phil" question and answer.

"I like the way you handled that," he said.

He read the others, nodding and taking bites of his food. One questioner was concerned about putting her mother in a nursing home versus bringing in a nurse to provide home care. After making a few comments both pro and con, Beth suggested the person pray about the decision. *That was wise,* Ross thought, *rather than pretending she had all the answers and leaving herself open for criticism.* He nodded. "The prayer angle on this one puts the ultimate responsibility back on the person with the problem. That's good," he said, laying the paper aside.

Suppose she didn't think his question serious enough to answer? He didn't think it necessary to pray about it— he'd just have to take matters into his own hands. And no time like the present.

"Before you start work, I want to show you something," Ross said.

Right after breakfast, he led her up the hallway, through the foyer, and out the front door. He spread his hands and watched her expression.

"They're out," she said, her gaze taking in the profusely blooming cherry trees in his yard and the others lining the street on both sides. "I've wanted to see this since I was a little girl. Oh, how beautiful."

"Yes," he said, "very beautiful." He swept her up, putting one hand on her waist and taking the other, spinning them around in a dancing movement, before he drew her near while breaking off a small twig lavish with cherry blossoms.

They laughed together. The feel of her warmth against him, her soft small hand in his, and the mental image of her head thrown back with her hair swaying softly around her face while he held her close stayed with him all day long.

He hadn't wanted to let her go. But she took the twig, buried her nose in its sweet fragrance, and stepped back. "This afternoon," he said impulsively, "I'll take you to the Washington Monument. It's surrounded with cherry blossoms. We can go to the observation platform that's five hundred feet high and look down on the cherry trees. In fact," he added, "we can look out over the entire District of Columbia and sections of Maryland and Virginia."

She'd agreed that she would love it. He felt rather breathless just thinking about it, and the day dragged. She hadn't protested when he'd put his arms around her. What might she permit, seeing cherry trees as far as the eyes allowed?

As soon as he returned home, earlier than usual, she was all smiles and excitement. "Jacobs has agreed to go with us as soon as you returned."

"Ducky," Ross said, glancing at Jacobs, who shifted his gaze toward some distant object but looked quite pleased with himself.

Ross had to admit the excursion turned out to be quite fun, experiencing Washington from the eyes of someone who hadn't before seen the sights that he had grown up with. After visiting the monument, the three of them ate in an out-of-the-way place, and Ross found Beth's depiction of Small Town, USA, as interesting as she found his hometown. As they headed back to Rossiter House, Ross wondered when he would again have a private moment with this intriguing young woman. He had to admit that he had never

known anyone quite like Beth, and he couldn't wait to get to
know her even better.

❧

In Tuesday's paper, Ross recognized his question in Beth's
column.

> *Dear Auntie,*
>   *I've met this fabulous girl who is different from any
> I've ever known. She's the type you take seriously and
> go slowly with. I'm being a gentleman. She's not one
> to rush into things. But my time with her is limited.
> She will be leaving soon. Do I make a move—if you
> know what I mean?*
>   *No Time To Take It Slow.*

Ross tried to remain expressionless, but it was hard not
to laugh at the silly way he'd worded his own letter. Still,
he couldn't chance anyone suspecting he'd written to
"Auntie." Quickly, he skimmed over Beth's response.

> *Dear NTTTIS,*
>   *Let her know! Don't let this girl go without express-
> ing your feelings. Pray about it!*
>   *Auntie*

Ross read over the letter again. "Pray about it?" he questioned. "You think that's the answer this 'NTTTIS' wants?"
  She looked surprised. "Am I supposed to tickle their
ears in this column? Or give the answer I believe in?"
  "I don't mean that at all, Beth. I can understand your
saying pray about cancer or some other big issue. But
this? No!"

"This comes straight from the Bible," she said, not backing down. "We're told to pray without ceasing—about everything." Her color heightened as she spoke her mind. "But no, that's not my pat answer. Read the next one."

He did. In this one she admonished the woman to give her heart to Jesus—then pray about it.

"We'll get complaints on that one," he said. "Anybody with a brain acknowledges there's a God. But 'Jesus' gets them stirred up."

"I only know of one God," she said quietly, "and that's the one whose Son says there is no way to reach God except through Jesus. I don't know any trivial answers to life's questions. I pray about my answers and respond the way I believe God wants me to. The answer to life's problems are found in the Bible. If I'm not to respond according to my beliefs then—"

"No!" Ross interrupted. He didn't like the way this conversation was turning into an argument. He'd had in mind getting closer to her—not alienating her altogether. "I'm not saying that you shouldn't answer in your own way. I'm just. . .having a conversation."

Jacobs, who had remained quiet during the discourse, gave Ross a skeptical look, then addressed Beth. "Your replies are perfect, Beth. Keep up the good work."

Ross wasn't so sure, but he doubted too many people took the "Ask Auntie" column all that seriously. He lifted his hands in a gesture of surrender and laughed lightly. "Jacobs is editor in chief—and my advisor—so if he says it's 'perfect' then I concur." *After all,* he thought, *at the end of the column is printed a disclaimer that the responses by Auntie are not necessarily the views of the paper.*

Soon the conversation turned to other topics. Beth was

smiling at him again. He didn't agree that you had to pray about everything, but he admired her stand and respected her even more for not backing down when he questioned her. She reminded him of his dad in that respect. His dad would rather lose his Senate seat than compromise his faith.

Ross inwardly scolded himself for writing the letter. It had been an impulsive, ridiculous thing to do. He'd just wanted to feel her out on what she'd say. Now he knew. But it really didn't apply to them. Two consenting adults could have the kind of private life they wanted. And he felt ashamed, admitting to himself that the phrase "making a move" could be interpreted in more ways than one and sounded crass.

Later in the day, he read her response again. He'd never intended to treat her disrespectfully, and he was sure he hadn't. As he thought, it suddenly occurred to him that there probably was no better way to show a woman respect than to invite her to dine with your parents.

He had no intention of doing anything against Beth's will. He was taking things slowly, getting to know her. He liked her, and she seemed to like him. A grin began to slowly spread across his face. Of course he knew what Catherine had in mind. Catherine—who had introduced the right girl to the right guy more than once. So, she had in mind matching up her niece with him.

Jacobs too, had said more than once that Ross had better think about settling down with the right woman if he expected to have political ambitions.

Ross snorted and shook his head. Not yet. He remembered the line of a song he'd heard years back. "Girls just wanna have fun."

Well, Catherine, Jacobs, Beth—sometimes guys just wanna have fun.

ঝ

Stimulated! That's how Beth felt about the discussion with Ross. She hadn't even thought of his being the owner of the paper and she being the employee. He and Jacobs treated her like a friend, or one of the family, with whom they could be honest.

And it wasn't that Ross wasn't a believer. He had stated a fact that she knew to be true. People threw the name of God around as if it were a byword and resented the name of Jesus. But Christians weren't supposed to be silent about their beliefs. They were to tell the Good News of Jesus to everyone.

It occurred to her that she and Bob never argued—not even about something as important as the ring he said he wanted to put on her finger. He'd said he couldn't afford it yet, and she accepted that. Looking at her fingers, she wondered if she really wanted that ring on her finger.

She never surprised Bob, and he never surprised her.

But Ross was a different matter. Just a word could set him off—like later that evening when he said he'd like for her to have dinner with his parents. He'd mentioned the idea to them, and they were eager to get to know her.

"I'll cook," Beth said.

"Cook?"

Beth couldn't help but laugh. "Ross, you sound like Greta when she doesn't understand a certain English word."

He looked skeptical. "It's just that I've never invited a girl to dinner and had her offer to cook. Frankly, I doubt that I know anyone, except chefs, who can cook. My mom used to, but she fixes meals rarely since Dad became a senator and she's required to host so many dinners. I mean, caterers or employees prepare the meals."

"Okay," she conceded, "if you don't think they'd like an informal dinner of southern fried chicken, biscuits, gravy, mashed potatoes made with milk, butter, and mayonnaise, corn on the cob, green beans almondine, and pecan pie with ice cream for dessert."

"How soon can you have it ready?" he asked.

❧

Two days later, Beth wondered how she could ever have been confident enough to try and cook for a senator and his wife. But maybe they wouldn't know if it turned out horrible. Maybe they'd never eaten southern food.

Her nervousness vanished, however, after she, herself, helped Trudy serve, and sat down to accolades, followed by second helpings of just about everything.

During his second piece of pie, the senator turned to his wife. "There's a party next week at Capitol House," Clement Rossiter said. "I think it's time we introduced Catherine's niece to Washington society as well as some of our friends."

"I quite agree," Gayle Rossiter said. "I even told Catherine I intended to do that, but I've been so busy. You're right, our friends need to meet this young lady who has been giving advice and showing up in the newspapers lately."

The evening flew by, and soon the senator and his wife said their good-byes, repeating their thanks for a lovely meal.

After they left, Ross said, "They loved you."

"Oh, I hope so," Beth replied. "They're such wonderful people."

"There are a few matters of protocol we'll need to go over before the party," Jacobs said. "A matter of to whom you address as 'Your Excellency' or 'Mr. President.' That sort of thing. Also when to bow, shake hands, or curtsey."

"Oh dear," she said, wringing her hands. "I hope I have the appropriate dress to wear."

Jacobs smiled. "I'm sure Catherine would have seen to that," he said with conviction.

Beth returned his smile. "You like my Aunt Catherine, don't you, Jacobs?"

Jacobs managed to smile, but he didn't answer her question. It was one he had avoided for years, and he wasn't about to let Catherine's niece examine an issue he'd intentionally ignored.

❧

Beth stopped working in the early afternoon on Friday in order to ready herself for the party. After a luxurious warm bath, she rubbed perfumed lotion on her body until her skin felt smooth and soft and smelled like fragrant rose petals. She washed her hair and blow-dried it the way they had at the beauty salon where Aunt Catherine had taken her for a cut.

The gown she chose to wear was a soft silk of deep blue that made her eyes greener and her dark hair shine with golden lights. Her magnolia-like complexion needed no makeup, but she applied light blush for the evening and black mascara to her lashes and arched eyebrows.

"I wonder if I look like Washington society?" she asked herself as she stared at the girl in the mirror. She blushed at the reflection. She'd never looked so well, but compared with high society, she felt uncertain. She turned, and the dress moved softly with her movement, then fell in perfect lines to the floor.

Aunt Catherine had offered Beth the use of her jewelry and furs, saying they would compliment the dress. Beth had protested, but her aunt had packed them along with Beth's clothes. "Of course you can use them," the older woman had said. "You have two months of adventure ahead of you. Now make the best of it."

Beth fastened Aunt Catherine's diamond necklace around her neck, matching the bracelet that lay gracefully at her wrist below the long sleeve of the dress. Tiny matching diamonds graced her earlobes.

She took Aunt Catherine's white, floor-length mink from the closet.

Jacobs and Ross, handsome in formal attire, stood in the foyer and watched Beth descend the staircase.

"You'll be the belle of the ball," Jacobs said.

"Are you sure everything is all right?" she asked uncertainly.

"Fabulous," Ross said, and reached for the fur. He held it for her to slip into.

☙

At Capitol House, Beth was pleased with the hostess, and she could well imagine her Aunt Catherine shining in that role. The president was in attendance, behaving like any other partygoer, laughing and joking. She didn't even have to remember much of the protocol briefing Jacobs had given her.

The First Lady remembered her and began telling her how much she liked the column and particularly appreciated the element of faith. No kings and queens were present, but Gayle Rossiter, Ross's mother, introduced Beth to senators and their wives. The women apparently all read

Catherine's column and felt Beth was following in her footsteps quite well.

After much food and conversation, Senator Rossiter
approached Beth and asked if he could talk with her about
a project he had in mind.

"Oh, certainly," Beth replied.

He led her to a couch along one side of the spacious
room, where a few people passed and spoke but didn't
intrude on their conversation.

"You may think this is not a time to talk business, young
lady. But believe me," the senator said pointedly, "sometimes a lot more business takes place in gatherings like this
than on the Senate floor."

Beth laughed. "I don't mind."

"My father kept notes on his various visits to different
part of the world. You may know he was a foreign ambassador for two terms."

Beth nodded. "I've heard of him."

"He left his personal files in a mess. Some thoughts are
scribbled on paper napkins even. Some are hand scrawled.
The handwriting is atrocious. But he was a brilliant man
with important things to say and made a real difference
in the world. Now, I'm wondering: Do you suppose you
might at some time, without jeopardizing your position
with the paper, see if you can make some sense of them?
If so, they might end up being his memoirs."

"I would be honored to try, Senator Rossiter. Really, I'd
be thrilled. I so admire what I've heard of him. And you—
especially your Christian stand on moral issues."

He patted her hand. "Thank you, my dear. I'll have a
tractor trailer deliver the papers."

"Trac—" Beth began, her eyes wide.

The senator laughed. "Just kidding. I only said that so you wouldn't be overwhelmed when you get several boxes."

She laughed too. Then he said if they were to be collaborators she should call him Clem in private, like his friends did.

Beth smiled and thanked him, but she felt like pinching herself. What other surprises could possibly be awaiting her during this two-month adventure?

fourteen

Beth left Capitol House after midnight, feeling like a permanent Cinderella, who might never lose her slipper. In the cool, cherry-fragrant night, Ross led her to the limo in front. Jacobs had said he needed to stay behind for awhile.

"A month ago, I would never have believed this," Beth said dreamily, as she and Ross sat close in the darkness of the limo, one of the few times they had been alone together. " I sat in the Sunday school class with the president of the United States, had a conversation with his wife, I'm writing a column for a Washington paper, I was asked by a senator to sort out his dad's memoirs, and then asked to call him by his first name."

Ross's arm that was resting along the back of the seat came around her, and he lightly drew her to him. "You forgot to mention that you're riding in a limo with a future senator."

Beth didn't attempt to look away. She spoke as seriously as he. "I thought I was riding with the future president of the United States."

Ross's face was very close to hers in the darkened backseat of the limo. Their lips were saying one thing, but it seemed their eyes were saying another. Their eyes held. He didn't want to move away. His glance fell to her lips, softly parted, and lifted to her eyes, a strange glow in them. No, he didn't want to take advantage of a young woman caught up in a world of glamour and people of power and position. It was second nature to him, but new to her.

But on the other hand, she was an adult. They were both adults. And if adults were consenting. . .

The driver opened the door of the limo, and Ross realized they had arrived back at his house.

Neither said anything once they were in the stillness of the shadowy inner foyer. *Finally,* Ross thought, *the two of us are alone, without the watchful eyes of Jacobs.* It should have been this way all along. She was twenty-five, he was thirty-two. The idea of a chaperone was preposterous. But that was all a part of Catherine's plan, wasn't it? Make him wait. Make him stare at the cookie jar until he couldn't resist reaching for it.

Beth must feel it too. She didn't say good night and go up to her room. Instead, she paused in the foyer, as if waiting for him to make a move. He watched her go down the hall and into the office, where the darkness swallowed her up.

৯

Beth pushed the red button and listened to her messages. One was from her parents, just wanting to keep in touch. Another was from Bob, saying he loved her. Catherine called, telling her the columns were perfect, even better than she could have done herself. Beth picked up the receiver, then placed it back on the cradle. She was not ready to let this night end.

Her breath came shallow when she heard, or sensed, footsteps on the carpet. "Beth," she heard and turned, feeling the soft swish of silk at her ankles. Ross had removed his jacket and bow tie. He came nearer, a dark shadow silhouetted by the faint light from the hall. The red light throbbing on the answering machine intermittently stroked his handsome face. But any thought of danger was far removed from her mind.

She welcomed the coolness, like a fan touching her warm skin, when he took the fur and tossed it toward a chair. When he caressed her shoulders, her arms, her neck, her back, and her waist, it was as if she had been asleep for a long time, and her skin tingled with the awakening of his hands.

"I've been to those dinners a hundred times," he said, "but I've never enjoyed an evening like that more. You have a way of making me see things as if it's for the first time. And I want you to know, despite our disagreement about the column, I do respect your beliefs."

Beth felt lost in his gaze. When he added, "There's something I want to tell you," in a low, serious tone, her pulse raced. Her instinct was to lift her arms and raise her face to his. The look on his face told her that's what he wanted too.

The sudden blinding flash of light was like someone had dumped her into a tub of ice water. The voice of Jacobs followed. "I didn't realize you two were in here."

Ross stepped back, moving his hands from her shoulders. Beth placed hers against the edge of the desk she sat back against.

"I was just about to tell Beth," he said as Jacobs walked farther into the room, "that I'm going to Kosovo for a couple of weeks."

Was that really what he had been about to say?

What else? she reprimanded herself. She turned and stared at the still-blinking "I love you" message from Bob.

"I hope you have a good trip," Beth said, retrieving the

fur and adding, "Good night. I'll see you in two weeks."

She hurried from the room, wondering how she could have responded to Ross the way she had with Bob's words, "I love you," right there on the answering machine.

She tried telling herself this was just a fairy-tale ending to a magical evening. But she knew that dressing up and dinners and position were not the most important things in life—and that all those things had the power to corrupt. She'd just had a weak moment, that's all.

A weak moment?

How often she'd heard that excuse and inwardly condemned it. As she went into her bedroom and began changing into pajamas, she forced her thoughts away from Ross and to Bob. She hadn't really missed Bob. She hadn't wished he were in Washington with her.

And yet, hearing Ross saying he was leaving for two weeks—she missed him already.

What did that say about her relationship with Bob?

After she crawled into bed and turned out the lamp, her muddled thoughts remained. She closed her eyes, but could still feel the touch of Ross's hands on her shoulders, the look in his eyes, the acceleration of her own heartbeat.

What would "Auntie" have to say about this?

Pray about it!

≈

Beth was glad that the cardboard boxes of the ambassador's memoirs were delivered on Monday morning. She needed to keep busy every moment. She and Jacobs went to church on Sunday. They conversed about everything as usual, such as her columns, the political news, what her parents were doing, how Bob was grading a lot of final papers and planned to teach in Bible school at their church during the summer. She finished her columns by Wednesday, getting them ready to be typed.

She worked on the memoirs in her sitting room. The house was lonely without Ross. She had loved being with Jacobs, feeling a bond with him from the very beginning. Sometimes she would find him looking at her in strange ways. Not uncomfortable ways. Sometimes there seemed to be the kind of affection she saw in his eyes when he had joked around with Ross. At other times, it was a look of incredulity, as if he couldn't quite believe her.

Was it because he'd seen her and Ross so close together? Did he suspect her feelings for Ross threatened to go beyond friendship? Did he think that was a betrayal of her boyfriend?

Several times a day, when she allowed herself to think about it, she told herself not to take it personally. Jacobs was an important man, the editor of a large newspaper, an advisor to both a senator and an up-and-coming politician, and he met with the senator's campaign manager or had talks with him on the phone almost daily. He was a busy man. He was an important man. Maybe she was just in the way. Maybe Catherine should never have left her here and gone off to the Caribbean.

As if he sensed her concerns, on Wednesday morning after devotions and his prayer, Jacobs placed his hand on hers. "Beth," he said. "I know I've been preoccupied. But I want to tell you again how much your presence here means to me. Don't ever doubt that."

The warmth she saw in his eyes touched her heart. He was a dear man. She moved her hand from beneath his, went over to Jacobs, put her arms around him, and kissed his cheek.

There was something very touching about a grown man, important in the life of Washington, D.C., and who hobnobbed with senators, kings, queens, and presidents, but still had a heart tender enough to bring tears to his eyes.

fifteen

On Thursday morning, Beth's world turned topsy-turvy. Since neither Ross nor the senator were available, the campaign manager called, saying he desperately needed Jacobs's advice, so Jacobs went to the headquarters.

Around ten o'clock, Millicent got a call from a nursing home, saying her ninety-year-old mother had fallen while trying to pull herself up at her walker and was taken to the hospital.

Even in her concerned state, Millicent managed to give Beth some instructions on how to reach her or Jacobs in case of an emergency and asked if Beth could sit at her desk and take calls.

"What if it's not an emergency but still urgent?"

"You can handle it," Millicent replied.

"I'm glad to help in any way," Beth said. "I'll be praying for you and your mother."

"Thanks," Millicent replied as she hurried out the door.

The phone rang immediately. The message didn't sound urgent, so Beth said that she would have Jacobs return the call when he returned to the office. The next call sounded more urgent. "The report Mr. Jacobs has been expecting is being delivered by special courier. Please see that he gets this material right away. He's been expecting it."

"Yes, I will," Beth assured at the same time Trudy was thanking someone at the door, saying, "I'll give this to Mr. Jacobs."

"I believe it's here now," Beth said to the caller.

"I'll hold on while you make sure."

Beth met Trudy at the office door, then returned to the phone to tell the caller the envelope was from the National Investigative Service.

"That's it, thank you."

Beth laid the package on the desk while answering another call. The large, white envelope looked official and important. Since it was hand-delivered by special courier, accompanied by a phone call, she wondered if she should call Millicent. But Millicent had enough on her mind. Maybe she should call Jacobs. She'd supposed Millicent often had to make such decisions about what was important and what could wait. This appeared important. But so was Jacobs's meeting.

Maybe she should take a look. She felt sneaky considering that option, but if the contents were of great importance, a lot of damage could be done by delays. Well, she was filling in for the secretary, so she should act like one and use her best judgment.

After that mental lecture, she opened the envelope. This seemed urgent. If it was classified information, she'd just have to ask to be shot. She would take a peek, and if it didn't seem urgent, she'd leave it alone.

Now that was strange. On the first sheet, at the very top, below the letterhead of the investigation firm was her own name "Mary Elizabeth Simmons, commonly called 'Beth.' " Her initial surprise was replaced by a realization that anyone working in the Rossiter home should be checked out. This didn't appear urgent at all, just general information.

Should she?

Should she not?

She put it down. She picked it up. Maybe the papers weren't urgent. But there was an urgency inside her saying, *Read it.*

She wasn't sneaking; she was simply reading about her own life.

Yep! That was her all right. She had forgotten some of those awards she'd gotten. She smiled, remembering that she'd been homecoming queen in high school. In college, she'd concentrated on her studies and won a couple of writing prizes. She was proud of the journalism award she'd won in the state for an article on "Flag-Waving vs. Flag-Burning."

Yes, they got that right. She was on the "waving" side.

She turned to the last page. That's when she saw it.

No! She sank into the chair.

It wasn't true.

Where would that kind of information come from— dates, places, times, names?

A detective agency claimed to have obtained it.

No, she would not look at anymore. Quickly she stuffed the papers back into the envelope.

It was a lie!

She was not. . .adopted!

After slipping the papers back into the envelope, Beth stared at it while answering calls. It was as if she had been switched to cruise control, continuing to travel down the workday highway at a reasonable speed, pretending there were no obstacles on the road.

When the phone stopped ringing, she thought of Millicent. She'd promised to pray. She did. "And Lord," she added, "help us to correct this erroneous information in that envelope."

After awhile, however, she again took the papers from the packet and read them carefully. She became oblivious to the ringing phone, allowing the answering machine to pick up the calls.

Of course, she wasn't adopted. But just suppose it was true? Millions of people were adopted. She knew several in her own hometown and even had a friend at church who was adopted, but hers was a family like anyone else's. It was no sin to be adopted—in fact, it was just the opposite. An adopted child was chosen, deliberately, and usually waited and sacrificed for.

My parents waited years for me.

Adoptive parents definitely wanted their child.

My parents have always called me their "miracle child."

Adopted children would not be taken for granted because they'd been hard to come by.

My parents couldn't have any more children, they said.

But if she were adopted, why did she look like her mother's side of the family? Everybody said she was the spitting image of. . .of Aunt Catherine.

That must be some sort of coincidence. After all, people chose to see parental characteristics in newborn babies when most of them looked like Eskimos to her. She continued reading.

Catherine!

Cold chills ran up Beth's spine. All reason seemed to have left her, and she wanted to go out for a run. But she had to do something first. She took a scrapbook off a shelf and placed it on her desk. Several of her serious letters had questions about adoption. One had appeared in the paper last week. She opened the scrapbook where she was keeping all of her columns.

Dear Auntie,

What can a middle-aged woman do who has made a mess of her life? She gave up her child when it was born and now she wants to be a part of her life. She wants her to know. The child is an adult now. Would it be right to break this news to the unsuspecting child who has had a wonderful life and loves her parents? She has a strong faith in God. Could she handle such information, or should she remain unsuspecting?

Confused

Beth had given that question a lot of thought and prayer. Was it coincidence that such a question was raised while Jacobs had in his hands an erroneous report? Taking a deep breath, Beth read her own answer to "Confused."

Dear Confused,

I think the kind of adult you describe, who loves her parents and has a strong faith in God, would be delighted to know the birth mother who has such a strong desire to acknowledge her. I don't see that the truth would take anything from the adopted person, but could add another person to her life to love. It might be wise, however, to alert the parents first, even though the adopted person is an adult.

Be sure and give your heart to Jesus, so the Holy Spirit can help you make a final decision as you pray.

Love,
Auntie

sixteen

When Jacobs returned after eleven, Beth told him about Millicent's having to leave because of her mother. "You have several messages, but I was distracted by the report that came. I thought it might need your immediate attention, so I looked at it." With an unsteady hand, she handed the envelope to Jacobs.

A concerned look crossed Jacobs's face as he looked down at the envelope. He sat at his desk and took out the papers. The first pages were the same as he'd received before. The third indicated that there were no close relatives of the Simmons from whom Beth could have been adopted. The final page was about Catherine's whereabouts twenty-five years ago and that she had given birth to a baby at a hospital in California.

Jacobs's hands shook as he tried unsuccessfully to return the papers to the envelope. He grew pale and took several deep breaths before looking at her in a strange way. He didn't say it was an error. He spoke as if the report were correct. "You had no knowledge of this?"

Beth shook her head. She felt as if she were existing in some kind of vacuum and it was her choice how to feel. No feelings came. She was numb—as if her emotions had ceased to function.

Her mind was working overtime, however. So many unclear thoughts were battling around in Beth's head. She could not understand—even if the adoption was a fact—

why it was a matter to be investigated or to be of concern to Jacobs. Without any protest from Jacobs, she returned to the library and picked up the phone.

She could get this straightened out right away. She called Pamela's home phone and talked with her briefly. After hearing what Pamela had to say, Beth felt she had no choice but to call Catherine.

"Aunt Catherine," she said after she listened to the woman's small talk about the weather in the Caribbean being heavenly and her excursions being glorious, "have you been reading my columns?"

"Yes, darling. Don't you remember how I complimented your responses? I even said the paper might replace me with you. Which would not disturb me at all. The only reason I've kept on with that is because I haven't found anyone who had enough sense to do it well. Those I've interviewed were either overqualified and responded with psychological discourses that no one could understand or were so lacking in common sense that they didn't know which end was up. Now, darling, don't tell me you have a problem."

"Yes, yes I do," Beth said, hearing the choppiness in her voice. "Did you read the one from the woman asking about telling her grown, unsuspecting child that she is adopted?"

"Well, yes, Beth. I told you. I've read them all. And I agreed with your answer."

"Well, I was wondering if there is a way to follow up and discover if the questioner took my advice, and if so, what the results were. Wouldn't it be interesting to do an article on how the advice column has helped others?"

Beth heard the hesitation in Catherine's voice as she answered, "All names and address of the questioners are kept and filed away for future reference in case a problem occurs. Pamela clips everything together and gives them to Jacobs's assistant to put in a confidential file."

"Yes, that was my understanding," Beth replied. "I asked Pamela about this one, and she said it was in a stack that you felt important to answer but that there was no name and address attached. Although names and addresses are required, she let it pass because you apparently intended to respond to it."

"Beth?" Her aunt's response sounded like a question.

Beth said nothing. She did not know how to fill such an awkward silence. "I wonder," she said, hardly able to speak over the tightness in her throat, "do you suppose that woman took my advice?"

After an even longer pause, Aunt Catherine asked in a trembling voice, "Is Jacobs there?"

Not knowing how to respond to her aunt's evasiveness, Beth slowly hung up the phone.

Staring at the "Ask Auntie" column, she thought of how glib her answer had been. As if a person could be told, "You've been lied to for twenty-five years," and come out of the experience unscathed.

❧

Catherine called right back. The phone kept ringing until the answering machine took over with that awful politeness that grated on her nerves. What could she, should she, say to Beth? She had to talk to Jacobs. When he picked up, she demanded, "What's going on, Jacobs? Beth called, asking about adoption."

His voice was strained. "Did you know that Beth is adopted?"

Catherine gasped. "How do you know?"

"It's in the investigative report," came his bland reply.

Catherine's voice was frenzied. "You really had Beth investigated?"

"It's normal procedure, Catherine. She saw the report by mistake." His voice held incredulity. "You're her mother, Catherine."

Catherine didn't answer. He hadn't asked. He'd told her. In a stilted voice he said, "There's one thing missing from the report."

Catherine held her breath. She'd been silent about this for more than twenty-five years. What could she say now? What could she say to Jacobs?

Words were as difficult for him as for her. "You know what a scandal this will be if it comes to light."

"I've always known," she said with a sob in her voice.

Jacobs, who had never said a cross word to her before, ordered gruffly in a manner she dared not disobey, "Catch the next flight home."

❧

Catherine stared at the column and the advice Beth had given. "Did the woman in the column take my advice?" Beth had asked. Catherine prayed, *God, I need You more than I've ever needed You in my life. Except that day when Mary Elizabeth took my baby in her arms and Beth became hers. I named her after the best person I knew—my older sister. And I gave away my baby. Because I loved her. Because I thought it was best for everyone.*

"Give your heart to Jesus," Beth had said. Catherine's mind tumbled back over the years. Mary had called to tell Catherine that Beth had given her heart to Jesus. Catherine flew home for the celebration of Beth's beginning her life as a Christian. Beth had asked, "Are you a Christian, Aunt Catherine?"

"Oh, honey," she had said. "I sure believe in God. And I pray every day. For you, too."

Beth wasn't satisfied with that answer. "You have to believe in Jesus too, if you're going to be a Christian."

"Yes, darling, I believe that."

"Well, you can't just believe. You have to ask Jesus to come into your heart."

Catherine had nodded. "You're absolutely right. And I'm so pleased you've done that. This is the most important day of your life, Beth. I'm so proud of you."

Give your heart to Jesus.

That's what her little girl had said. Catherine had always believed. She'd believed just as much and just as intensely as Mary Elizabeth. But how could she give her heart to Jesus, when she'd already given it to Mary Elizabeth Simmons? She'd given away her little girl, her flesh and blood, the offspring of the love of her lifetime.

Give her heart to Jesus?

She had no heart after that. Just an empty, blank spot. Something kept beating in there. But it felt like a whip that made a new scar with each stroke. She'd never become immune to the pain. She'd just accepted it, pasted a smile on her face, and acted as if she'd deliberately chosen a career because it appealed to her more than a husband and family life. She'd acted well. She was happy-go-lucky Catherine, without a care in the world.

Give my heart to Jesus?

She was sorry, but the old one was crushed. And now, had she committed the greater sin of having crushed the heart of her child, whom she loved more than anyone? Could even Jesus straighten out the mess she'd made? Did He want the life of a lonely woman living under the façade of an independent, carefree lifestyle?

Jesus, all I have is a crushed, battered, beaten-up old piece of a heart. You'd have to give me a new one before I could even attempt to give it back to You.

❧

Although Beth kept telling herself she wasn't adopted, she had to accept the possibility. Soon after she'd talked with Aunt Catherine, Jacobs had come in to say her aunt would be returning from the Caribbean on the next flight out. "Do you want to talk?" he asked, adding, "Or I'd be glad to sit with you or take a drive or something."

She shook her head. "I'm just kind of numb about the whole thing. Anyway, if it turns out to be true, it's no crime to be adopted. And besides, it's not your crisis, it's mine."

His glance darted away from her and back again. "What affects you, Beth, affects me. I'll be right in there if you need me."

"Thank you," she said. "I think I do need you to be there." She returned his warm smile. "Right now, I just want to try and absorb this."

He nodded and returned to his office.

She decided not to talk with her parents or Bob on the phone until after she felt more accustomed to the whole idea and the matter was settled between herself and Aunt Catherine. Later, she would E-mail them and pretend everything was just super. After all, regardless of the facts Aunt Catherine might disclose, Beth was a grown woman with her own life to live.

Suddenly her thoughts were interrupted by Jacobs's shout of, "Dead? What do you mean, dead?" She could only sit there, stunned. Then he was asking, "How? A plane crash? A shooting?"

Plane crash? Shooting? Who was dead? A terrible sense of dread swept through her as her stomach churned. Ross had flown to Kosovo, a dangerous place filled with fighting, and his schedule would then take him to the Sudan—an equally troubled spot on the globe.

She rushed to the open door and stopped. Jacobs was pacing with the phone to his ear and was demanding that somebody had better find out more information. Such statements had to be backed up with more than a newspaper correspondent's word. "Find out where, when!" he barked into the phone and then hung up.

Beth had never seen him so unglued as he looked at the phone and looked at her with disbelief written all over his face. This man who advised politicians and, as editor of a newspaper was supposed to see things objectively, was at a loss.

The ringing phone shook him out of it. "Gayle," he said, then closed his eyes as he listened. He nodded. "Yes, I heard. I'll be right there."

"That was Gayle Rossiter," he said, still holding the phone. "She said it's been verified." He swallowed hard, his gaze leveled at Beth, but she had the feeling he was seeing beyond her as he said the most dreaded words one could hear about a person they loved.

"He's dead."

seventeen

Ross stared out the window of the private jet, unable to distinguish a line between the gray sky above and the gray water below. There was no color in his life now, just the awareness of flying in a plane that carried the body of his dad.

He's dead.

How could it be real? They'd been warned of the danger of the militant regime in Southern Sudan. They'd heard stories of people who stepped out into the street and were killed by an exploding mine. Hospitals might be bombed at any time. Terrorists and shootings were a part of everyday happenings.

But that hadn't happened when he and his dad had gone into Sudan to try and give hope to the maimed and suffering at a hospital. They had returned safely, by helicopter, to Kosovo, where people faced life-threatening situations every day. Why didn't it happen there?

Instead, it happened in a luxury hotel in Paris. They'd gone to lunch in the hotel dining room. After returning to their room, the senator typed a few notes on his laptop about the successful trips to Kosovo and Sudan. Ross had leaned back in a chair and propped his feet up, thinking about how much more interesting Paris would be if Beth were there.

That's when it happened. His dad said his arm felt strange and commented it probably went to sleep before the rest of him. He'd laughed, then he gasped and grabbed his chest. Even as he lay in pain, he told Ross he loved him and was proud of him.

At the hospital, when it appeared he might be stabilized, he asked Ross to tell his mother he loved her. Just before the final attack, he simply said, "It's my time."

He hadn't seemed to mind, Ross thought. *He'd lived a good life and looked forward to going home to be with the Lord.*

But what am I without my dad?

He couldn't pose that question to Jacobs, his advisor. He'd alienated Jacobs before he'd left for Kosovo. But he knew how he was supposed to act. Go on and follow his dad's footsteps. Be his own man. Be strong for his mom.

How was he supposed to do that when, for the first time in his life, he was feeling an empathy with the orphaned children of Kosovo?

ঽঌ

Being adopted was the least of Beth's concerns in the days that followed. She called her parents and Bob, not about the adoption, but about the senator's death. Millicent's mother had asked why couldn't she, at age ninety, have been the one to go to her Maker instead of the good senator.

No one knew the answer, but Millicent had to take time off to get her mother established in a nursing facility after her hip operation. Beth filled in as best she could, busily taking and sending messages and handling the more routine inquiries.

Jacobs, in spite of the numerous arrangements and the loss of his dearest friend, took time to tell Beth that her aunt had returned and was staying with Gayle Rossiter.

"Catherine is Gayle's closest friend," Jacobs explained.

"However, Catherine asked me to assure you that you're her top priority and she'll come if that's what you want. She didn't call, because she thought you might not want to talk with her."

"I do," Beth said, "but not now. No one should be concerned with me right now. I'm here to help out in any way I might be needed."

"You're needed right here for the time being," he said, with a sad warmth in his eyes.

"I'm fine," she said. "Don't be concerned about me."

"That's a hard request to fill," he said as he put his hand on her shoulder and gave it a gentle squeeze.

Beth didn't want Aunt Catherine, Jacobs, or herself to think about her having gained a mom—when Ross had just lost a dad.

When the dazed-faced Ross came into Jacobs's office where she was sitting at Millicent's desk, she rose to meet him. He held open his arms, and she went into them, raising her face to his. "I'm so sorry. I wish I could do something—anything."

His eyes clouded over. She laid her head against his chest as he held her tightly and spoke brokenly against the top of her head. "It helps just knowing you're here, Beth."

She nodded against the beating of his heart. "I'll be praying."

"Thanks," he said, stepping back.

She watched him go, wishing she could go with him. Wanting to be a comfort to him. Wanting to be by his side at a time when he most needed someone. He'd thanked her when she said she'd prayed. *How could people grieve,* she wondered, *without the comfort and peace that only God could give?*

Jacobs had been dubbed, even by himself, as a man in control. He'd been Senator Rossiter's first campaign manager and had been credited with getting him elected years ago. Later, after the senator's life and record spoke for themselves, he'd worked more behind the scenes and become a senior editor, then editor in chief of the newspaper. He'd also concentrated on grooming Ross for politics.

Jacobs had always been able to keep private matters out of his mind while concentrating on the business at hand. He'd managed to keep personal, firmly outside the office doors, his agony at watching his wife suffer during her years with cancer. The Lord had given him the strength to bear that sorrow and then work through the grief that followed her death. He'd relegated the past to the past.

But the seven days since he'd learned of the senator's death had been more difficult than anything he'd ever known. Death was certain and final in this life. Several times, he'd had to face that reality and accept it. But now the man who had been his closest friend for most of his life was dead. Other than Gayle and Ross, no one had been closer to the senator, so Jacobs accepted the job of writing the newspaper articles about his friend that dominated the front page for days. At the funeral, Jacobs talked about the senator's exemplary life that, more than anything, reflected his commitment to the Lord.

After the services were over and people returned to everyday life, Jacobs faced several adjustments. Obviously the reelection campaign was over. He and Ross talked to all the avid supporters and employees, decided what to do with the funds, and closed up the headquarters. The feeling of grief and loss were ever-present with them both. Their feelings had to be put aside enough to come to grips with the present.

That young girl who had devotions with him in the mornings, who respected and liked him, had put aside her concerns during this time of the Rossiter family's needs. But she deserved explanations.

Only one person could give those.

Jacobs knew Catherine had returned to her Capitol House apartment after Gayle's mother had arrived and decided to stay on with the senator's widow after the funeral.

"I'm coming over," he said to Catherine. He decided to walk the few blocks, and along the way became increasingly aware that the pink cherry blossoms, that had so delighted Beth, were gone.

The butler let him in and said Catherine was expecting him in her second-floor sitting room. Jacobs ascended the stairs and, through the open doorway, saw her sitting in a chair opposite one where he would sit.

Her questioning look, as she started to rise but sat again, reminded him of another time. Questions must have been in her mind then too. She'd never asked them. He'd remained silent. For twenty-six years he'd remained silent about it, as had she, as if the event had never occurred.

As it had been then, it was now, his responsibility to speak.

He knew the answer. It was in the report. It was on her face. But he had to hear it.

"Catherine," he said when he sat in the chair opposite her, "are you Beth's mother?"

"Yes," came the affirmative reply from trembling lips set in a pale, stricken face.

He repeated to himself, *Beth is not Catherine's niece. She is Catherine's daughter.*

Stunned, his thoughts carried him to the inevitable conclusion. *That can mean only one thing: Beth is also my daughter.* He slumped back in his chair.

&

"I was not what I pretended to be," Catherine said, "just a girl out for a good time."

She wanted Jacobs to understand the truth about her, so she talked, omitting nothing, while he gazed at her with that intense expression, his elbow on the chair arm, and his fingers contemplatively against his lips.

She had been reared like her sister, a small-town girl with basic Christian beliefs. But she'd gotten away from that when she'd begun to be recognized as something of a beauty. She'd been Miss Magnolia and gone to Washington, D.C., to ride in the Cherry Blossom parade on a float. Secret Service was there, of course, posted at the hotel to protect all the young beauties from each state.

She'd always had beaus. Any boy she wanted would fall at her feet. All through college she didn't have a serious relationship with a young man. She was having too much fun flitting from one to another, receiving honors for her beauty, getting attention, making Mary Elizabeth jealous to distraction.

Finally, Mary Elizabeth met a good, basic Christian man, and she married him. By the time the festival came around, Catherine was becoming bored with it all—riding in parades, waving to the crowds. Then a tall, dark, handsome, newspaper man drew her attention. Eventually, she realized she'd seen him on TV, covering the news in foreign countries. Since he seemed to ignore her, she flirted with him outrageously, but to no avail.

The boys lost their appeal. She had no idea her heart could become entangled with anyone. It never had. Her background and training were in communications. She talked with Mr. Rossiter, the man's boss, and he gave her a trial job for three months. During that time she learned that Jacobs was dating an ambassador's daughter. But Catherine wanted him for herself. That's why she'd asked to go along with Jacobs when he was given an assignment to the south of France. She'd argued it would give her the opportunity to better learn the business.

Jacobs's sudden words startled her. "Catherine," he said kindly, "you don't need to go into details."

"Yes, Jacobs," she said, "I do. This is a time for truth. No more lies. They hurt too much."

She continued with her story.

Catherine had thought she wanted to make this man, who ignored her, pay attention. She needed to prove to herself that a man couldn't resist her. She'd never had the challenge of an older, handsome man. She truly thought all she wanted was a few stolen kisses, the arms of a real man around her. She told herself that. But deep inside, she knew better. She was spoiled, strong-willed, and had never cared for any of the boys around her. Here was a real man, one who resisted her—and that was a challenge. She pursued him relentlessly. Once his arms were around her, she never wanted to be free of them.

The following morning she wasn't proud of herself; it wasn't something she knew how to talk about, and before they had a chance to try, Jacobs told her he had been called back to Washington. He was being replaced by another reporter.

"I stayed on," she said. "And after two months had passed, I knew I was pregnant. But by that time the word was out that Mr. Rossiter had decided to run for the Senate, you were promoted to assistant editor of the newspaper and had been chosen to be Mr. Rossiter's campaign manager. When we received the newspaper about it, the article was accompanied by a picture of the two of you with the ambassador's daughter in the background."

Jacobs interrupted. "That's when you sent word to me that you wanted to stay in France as long as a reporter was needed or else be sent to other foreign countries."

Catherine nodded.

"I distinctly remember asking if you were sure that's what you wanted," he said.

"Yes," she said, "I was sure. I knew that my return to Washington in my condition would create a scandal. I could not do that to you. You would have to resign from being campaign manager. It would be splashed all over the newspapers that Rossiter's campaign manager had had an affair. It would ruin your future with the ambassador's daughter. It could even cost Clem Rossiter, whom I knew was a Christian man, his bid for the Senate."

Catherine tried to ignore that Jacobs now had his eyes closed and that his head slowly shook from side to side as if all this were unbelievable. Then he looked at her with eyes full of pain. "I never even considered that you—"

"I know," she said; "I never blamed you. I was young and innocent, yes. But I brought it on myself. You and others didn't need to suffer because of my self-indulgent behavior."

"I was married when you had the baby," he said.

Catherine's lips trembled. She mustn't cry. She'd never

cried so much in her life as when she looked at that picture of Jacobs and Patricia, he in a black tux, she in a white gown, each with a small piece of cake in their fingers, ready to feed each other. She'd read the article over and over. They were wonderfully matched. Patricia was no beauty queen, but she was lovely, educated, refined, and an ambassador's daughter.

After a thoughtful moment, Jacobs said, "You sent word that you wanted a month's leave. You had an ailing grandmother in California."

She nodded. "That wasn't true. About the 'ailing,' I mean. I went to stay with my paternal grandmother. My parents and maternal grandparents lived in South Carolina. I couldn't return to that small town, where I had been acclaimed as their celebrity, and embarrass myself and my relatives. I contacted a friend in California who worked with a San Francisco paper. She was more than eager to have me come and work for awhile, even after I told her I was pregnant."

Catherine and Jacobs sat in silence. How could she explain why she left her little girl? How could she tell this man that the only thing she had to remember him by, she had given away? But he was waiting.

Dear Jesus, she prayed silently, *You must have given me a new heart. Because something in my chest hurts so.*

However, she had to tell the rest of the story. When Catherine had mentioned the possibility of giving the baby up for adoption, her grandmother had contacted the rest of the family. "My parents, my sister, and her husband flew out to see me. I don't think they tried to sway me," Catherine said, "but all the possibilities got through to me."

Catherine had a career to think of. She wasn't the type

to be saddled with a baby. How could she support it anyway, since she said she could not return to Washington with a baby? She would lose her job.

Mary Elizabeth had been married for three years and had no children. She could never have a child. Mary Elizabeth was settled. She and John could give the baby a wonderful home life. They were active Christians, and Catherine felt like a rebellious sinner. She had nothing to give except embarrassment. And too, someone had mentioned, how many men would want to be saddled with another man's baby?

"I decided the issue before I ever saw my child," Catherine said. "I saw no future ahead for me and the child together except a life of struggle. She could have the best with Mary and John. I wouldn't have to endure the kind of scandal that would occur in Washington if I showed up there with a baby. And what would happen if I decided to quit the paper nine months after you and I had been working together? People had very suspicious minds. They would have done the math and drawn their own conclusions. Back then, I felt the eyes of the world were upon me and any move I made would be disaster for someone—especially for my unborn child."

"You made a great sacrifice, Catherine," Jacobs said.

She spoke over a raspy throat. "I didn't realize how great until I held her in my arms before her legal mother took her away." Forcing back her sobs, she continued. "I thought it best to pretend nothing had happened. So I returned to Washington. I intended to fall in love, marry, have children, and live a happy life like so many around me. But," she said, her voice dropping, as did her gaze, "I never found anyone else that I wanted in my life except my little girl, and the man I grew to love even more as I watched him become one of the most respected men in Washington."

Jacobs almost came out of his chair. "What are you saying?"

"That I loved you, Jacobs." She stared directly into his eyes. "Pity me. Hate me. Whatever. But this is my moment of truth. I cannot live with these dark secrets inside me anymore. It's like my life has been a walking lie."

eighteen

Jacobs had been ace reporter for the newspaper owned by Clement Rossiter II. They were also the best of friends. After an exhausting stint by Jacobs covering a war-ravaged, Middle Eastern country, Clement had laughed and said he knew what his friend needed to refresh him. He could cover the beauty pageant.

At first, Jacobs thought Clem was kidding, but Jacobs decided that the pageant would be a welcome assignment and maybe what he needed after having seen so much devastation and killing.

Right away, he was particularly drawn to Catherine, the beauty queen who won in the talent competition when she wore a patriotic costume—shorts of blue, tails of red-and-white stripes, shirt of stars, and a top hat of white with a band of red and white. She twirled a sparkling blue-and-silver baton with red-and-white tassels on it. She was a great hit in her high heels, prancing and twirling to the tune of "It's a Grand Ol' Flag."

She was a communications major and wanted to be a journalist. Jacobs had been thirty-five then, well into his career. He was quite taken with Catherine and was flattered with the attention she gave him. When Clement asked him, Jacobs agreed they should give her a chance at the newspaper. Although he had decided to ask Patricia to marry him, he relished the fact that he and the charming, witty, beautiful Catherine would be going to the south of France on assignment.

He quickly discovered that she had more than beauty. She had intelligence and journalistic ability. He wanted to teach her whatever she needed to learn. She seemed to think he was the greatest, and he was flattered. They worked, then they walked along the beach on the Riviera. He forgot his age of thirty-five and ignored hers of twenty-three as a full moon shone down upon them and the gentle waves caressed the beach.

Many nights, they stood in the shadows and forgot about anyone else but themselves. There was just the two of them, and one night after a moonlight swim they returned to their hotel but did not go to their separate rooms.

The following morning a phone call awakened them. While he was taking the call, she'd slipped out of bed and into her clothes and then left his room. There had been no time for discussion. His boss and best friend had been on the phone, telling him to take the next plane home. Clem Rossiter was going to run for state senator and wanted Jacobs to be his campaign manager.

Jacobs hadn't known what to say to Catherine. Would she be insulted if he apologized? Had he taken advantage of her? Was she sorry? He found her in the hotel dining room, eating breakfast and drinking coffee with some of the crew.

They all spoke when he walked up, and he sat in the empty seat across from her. She smiled at her coffee cup but didn't really meet his eyes, and he didn't know if she were afraid her happiness might show, or her embarrassment.

He told the crew he'd have to leave. He told himself it was just one of those things that happened when two people were attracted to each other. That's all it was. The haste of his new assignment and the excitement of it made him push everything else in the background. Besides, everyone was congratulating him, saying good-bye, making jokes by comparing the smog of Washington with the wide open spaces of the French Riviera. Catherine had smiled too, without even looking directly at him.

There had been neither time nor any need to say more to Catherine. He returned to Washington, and life became so hectic he tried not to even think of her. He was busy with the campaign and social engagements. When Catherine asked for foreign assignments, he felt inclined to give her whatever she requested.

As expected, he proposed to the ambassador's daughter, and Patricia began planning their wedding. He'd known for several years they were right for each other. They loved each other. She fit right in with his life, being the daughter of an ambassador, and he started becoming recognized by the powerful people in Washington.

And too, Catherine's reports were superb. He believed her to be caught up in her career. Apparently that night was simply a mistake that should be forgotten. After all, didn't a lot of people take their pleasure where they could with no regrets? He didn't have to try and make more of it than it was. He didn't like to think of it as a one-night stand, yet he didn't want to make more of it than it had been. A young girl caught up in the romance of the moment, with an older man who was her supervisor, her mentor. Had she been afraid not to give in to him? His conscience wouldn't allow him to treat it as something trivial to be dismissed.

His relationship with Patricia became tense. They both credited that to the hectic schedule of his additional responsibilities. The wedding plans continued. It was announced in the paper. Catherine would see it. The following day she called, saying there was to be a state wedding in Morocco and she'd like to cover it.

He told her yes. He was making such decisions, now that Clem was heavy into campaigning.

He never said, "Forgive me."

They simply went about their lives separately, and when she returned to Washington, he was totally committed to Patricia. Catherine never gave the impression she cared particularly about him, or anyone, except her career. She asked for the "Ask Auntie" advice column, and he gave it to her.

They ran in the same circles and often engaged in polite conversation. She became best friends with Gayle Rossiter. She never once gave the impression she was anything but a friend of his and Patricia's. Only one thing had changed about the Catherine he'd fallen for on the beach in the south of France. She never again turned challenging eyes his way, nor gave him a delighted smile.

She was polite and friendly. He'd come to accept that he had been a rapscallion who had taken advantage of a young girl infatuated with moonlight and sweet talk from an older man.

"Forgive me," he said now.

Catherine said, amid the tears bathing her face, "Something beautiful came from that night of indiscretion. Beth is something to be thankful for. She is a blessing."

Jacobs nodded, his own vision blurring.

A child.

My child.

I have a daughter. A lovely Christian girl.

His moment of overwhelming joy quickly changed as

questions bombarded his mind. Should Beth be told? If so, would her condemnation and rejection pierce his heart, causing a wound greater than if he'd never known the truth?

"What do we do now?" he asked helplessly.

"Let me talk to Beth," Catherine said. "I don't know if she is strong enough to endure finding out that she's adopted, losing the senator, and discovering you're her father. This may all be enough to send her back to South Carolina. Oh, Jacobs, I don't want to lose her again."

❧

The day of truth, Beth thought, when Jacobs told her he was going to talk with Catherine at Capitol House. She couldn't concentrate on her work, especially with Ross working in the office next to her. Schedules had been off for everyone during the past weeks anyway.

Ross just nodded when she told him she would be in her room for awhile.

She lay on the couch in her sitting room, trying to figure out how she would react if Aunt Catherine said, "Yes, I'm your birth mother."

Hearing a faint knock on her door, she sat up and said, "Come in." When her aunt walked in with that stark look on her face and concern in her eyes, Beth thought she knew the answer of who was her birth mother.

Aunt Catherine sat beside her and took her hands.

Beth listened to her story of how she had been a willful young woman who fell hard for a handsome man when she was on assignment in France. She hadn't thought much about the future or of consequences, only of what pleased her at the moment—and that had been being in the arms of the man with whom she was so infatuated.

"I did what I thought best at the time," Aunt Catherine said. "The man was becoming quite important on the political scene. I knew it would ruin his personal life and several persons' careers if it became known that I was pregnant with his child. He never knew. And I knew that I had just been a headstrong girl, pretending she knew all about life when she knew very little."

"That was a noble act, Aunt Catherine," Beth said.

Her aunt shook her head. "Not entirely. I can't say I was completely unselfish. In the back of my mind was the realization of guilt, shame, and shattered dreams. Mary Elizabeth was the good girl—I was the black sheep. I knew I couldn't pursue my ambitions. I would have to humble myself, struggle."

"You don't have to tell me all this," Beth said, when the older woman paused to wipe her eyes.

"I want to. I'm trying to be honest, but I honestly don't know exactly why I made all the decisions the way I did. Everyone thought the decision to let Mary and John adopt you was a good one. I truly wanted to do the right thing. But I can tell you this, without a shadow of a doubt."

She looked directly into Beth's eyes. "If I had seen you and held you before I signed those adoption papers, nobody could have pried you out of my arms, even with a crowbar."

She began to sob. Beth went over and put her arms around her shoulders, drawing her head close to her. "Don't cry, Aunt Catherine. I was shocked to find this out. But I'm not hurt. I'm the same person I've always been."

The woman lifted her head and moved back. "You don't despise me or think I'm a horrible person?"

"No." Beth shook her head. "I can't say if your decision was right or wrong. But I know I've had a good life with parents who love me, and I'm grateful for that. And I've had an aunt who I have loved and admired all my life." She smiled, in spite of the moisture in her own eyes. "I still do."

"Oh, honey. I think I've made a much better aunt than I would have a mother." They smiled affectionately at each other. "Now," Aunt Catherine said, "maybe we'd better get dried off and fix our faces."

"One more thing, Aunt Catherine," Beth said, as a thought dawned upon her. "You said if your pregnancy was known, it would have ruined careers. Is that still true?"

After a thoughtful moment, her aunt replied, "No. That's no longer true."

Beth got the impression that Aunt Catherine hadn't realized that before.

"Then I'd liked to call my parents and tell them I know about this. And Ross should know. I don't want to keep anything from him. He's been through enough lately."

Aunt Catherine nodded. "We'll be in the library."

nineteen

Beth came down to the library after talking with her parents, who were relieved that she knew and was apparently taking it well. Aunt Catherine was sitting on the couch and Jacobs in a chair. Ross was holding onto the back of the chair opposite Jacobs.

"Have you told him?" Beth asked, walking into the library. She sat near her aunt.

"Catherine just told me an incredible thing," Ross said, moving around to sit in the chair. "Is this true? Catherine, you're her mother?"

"It's true," the two women said in unison.

"Why now?" Ross asked. "Why tell her now, Catherine? I mean it's your business, but—"

Jacobs spoke up. "Beth found out by mistake. She saw the investigative report."

"I was shocked," Beth said. "But I'm glad I know. It doesn't bother me. I'm the same."

Ross shook his head and pointed at Catherine. "And at first, I thought you brought Beth here as a matchmaking scheme for me. I can truthfully say from the very beginning I never minded that idea."

"No, Ross. One of the primary reasons I brought Beth here was so she could get to know her birth father."

"My uh. . .what?" Beth asked, turning a stark gaze toward her aunt.

"Your birth father, Beth. I told you—"

Beth was shaking her head. "I haven't thought of a birth father. Even when you mentioned the man, I pictured in my mind a handsome French news reporter. Who? I mean, when do I meet him?"

Aunt Catherine stared at her as if in shock before slowly turning her head toward Jacobs.

"Jacobs?" Ross asked in disbelief, echoing what was in Beth's mind.

"Oh, no, not this way," Jacobs moaned.

Slowly Beth's eyes moved to Jacobs who, at some point in the conversation, had leaned forward, his elbows on his knees and his face in his hands.

"Neither of you knew this?" Ross asked.

"I found out this morning," Jacobs said wearily.

Beth continued to stare at Jacobs, as he now studied the floor. She was sure he wished it would open up and swallow him. That kind, dear man was her biological father? She opened her mouth to speak, but it was so dry, no sound came. What could she say, anyway?

Then Ross began to speak. "How could you be so thoughtless, Catherine? I admit, Beth is one fabulous girl, but this is not the way to drop something like this on her."

Fabulous? Beth could hardly believe she'd heard right.

Aunt Catherine began apologizing. She'd neglected to say Jacobs's name. It was all so clear to her as she had talked with Beth that she thought it was clear to Beth, too. "I make one mistake after another," she wailed. "I never learn. I give advice, but I have none for myself. You can't tell by my actions that I took your advice, Beth, but I did. I have turned my life over to the Lord. Oh, He has such a lot of work to do on me."

Give your heart to Jesus had been the advice she'd

given in the column, Beth remembered. But something else seemed to be pressing, pushing against her memory. *Fabulous*.

"Yes," Beth said to her aunt, struggling to appear as if this were a normal conversation, "I wrote that the person should turn her life over to Jesus. That's when Ross said it was all right to talk about God, but go easy on the 'Jesus' answers. They'd get complaints."

Fabulous! Her gaze moved to Ross. "That was the day a guy wrote in to ask how long he should wait to make his move on this fabulous girl."

Seeing his grimace and the guilt covering his face, she stated, rather than asked, "That was your question, Ross. But you didn't like my answer."

He swallowed hard. "Beth. Let me explain."

"No explanation is necessary," she said. Something caught in her throat.

She'd thought she could handle this. But now she fe the same way some people looked as they came off roller coaster—scared, frazzled, shaking, unable to g balanced footing in an unsteady world.

She stood, and the words just spewed out. "I don't kno you people," she said between shallow, audible breaths. came here at the request of my aunt, to see Washingt and write a simple little column. And now I find out you all fakes. You're not who you're supposed to be."

She looked from one stark face to another. "You tell n you're my mother. That's my father. And the future pre dent of the United States is a phony. And the column She scoffed, her voice rising. "This was my chance work with a big newspaper in a big city. How good t would look on a résumé. Well, I'll tell you. I'd rather in Henderson than stay one minute longer with people who have deceived me. Were all the questions for the column planted?"

Without waiting for an answer, she plunged on. "All of you need truth in your lives. If you go easy on Jesus, you go easy on the truth. I wish I'd never come here. I wish I'd never seen any of you. I can't stand it. I just can't stand it."

Aunt Catherine and Ross moved as if to come to her. "No, don't touch me," Beth said and put her hand out as a shield. "Get away."

She didn't feel like herself anymore. And according to Aunt Catherine, she wasn't. She'd thought the adoption didn't matter. But something deep inside was spilling over—just as the tears were now spilling from her eyes—and she seemed helpless to prevent either flood from happening.

"I thought all of you were the most wonderful people I'd ever met. You were good and honorable and in positions of power and influence. I've never liked the jokes about politicians. I never believed the majority of public-office holders were crooked and out for themselves.

"Now I discover that the people who set the best example weren't real. You all were wearing very attractive masks. I never want to see any of you again. I'm going home. Where I belong."

Jacobs got up and left the room. Ross walked over to a window, staring out. "Let me go with you," Aunt Cathrine said. "Or help you pack. Just let me explain."

"It's a little late for explanations. And as for packing, there's nothing here I want. The biggest celebration in Henderson is a cookout for the city council candidates. I wear blue jeans to that."

❧

Beth ran upstairs for her purse, then ran back down and out to the sidewalk. She waved her arms like Aunt Catherine had done before, but no cab appeared. The magic was gone. Then a car stopped. It was Fred. Someone behind her opened the back door of the car.

"Get in," said Jacobs. So much pressure was pushing against the dam inside her that it threatened to break. He climbed in after her. "The airport, Fred."

"You have more important things to do than chase after me," Beth said, but when he put his arms around her, she leaned her head against his chest and the dam burst.

Jacobs, the man who advised senators and probably presidents, spoke gently. "Go home, Beth. Talk to your parents. This is a hard thing for you to suddenly face. But remember—" He paused to straighten her back in her seat, offer his handkerchief, and tell her to wipe her face.

She did, taking a few deep breaths, then leaned back against the seat, her eyes closed.

"Remember," he said. "After you've given this some thought and you've accepted it, if you want to come back to Washington, I'm here to help you in any way. You'll still have a job. The contract is for two months, you know."

"Oh, Jacobs, I'm letting you down. You didn't know either."

His smile was kind. "No, no. Every one of us has let you down. This wasn't handled in the right manner. Catherine meant well. Maybe you'll see that after you've absorbed the facts. Just know that I'm here for you, Beth."

He sighed. "To tell the truth, I'd like to run away too. But for today, I'll only go as far as the airport and watch you do it."

She sniffed and gave a short laugh. "I think you're trying to tell me a person can't really run away."

"Sooner or later, we have to face ourselves, Beth. I'm learning that today. The hard way."

"I guess you're more shocked than I am," she said.

"From the moment I saw the word 'adopted' on your record, I couldn't figure out how that could be when you looked so much like Catherine. And my affair with Catherine was twenty-six years ago. I had to investigate further. I told myself that my immediate bond with you was because you were Catherine's niece and looked like her. Now I know it's much deeper, Beth. You are my—" he shook his head as if he still couldn't believe it.

"My daughter," he said and turned his head to look out the window. "No wonder I felt such an affinity for you from the moment I saw you."

If the hanky weren't soiled she would have offered it to him. Instead she placed her hand on his. He turned his over and held hers all the way to the airport.

twenty

Beth looked down upon the southland. Sitting so high in the sky, she could think more objectively. It was like looking at her overall situation—sort of like she supposed God must do. She saw her life, how good it had been. As much as she adored Aunt Catherine, she could only be grateful for the life Mary and John Simmons had given her. They were her parents in the truest sense of the word.

That Catherine had given birth to her instead of the woman she had grown up calling Mom changed nothing in how she viewed Mary Elizabeth Simmons: She had been and always would be Beth's mom. At the same time, something deep inside Beth wanted to be a part of Catherine's life. There was a bond she couldn't deny.

But she would just chalk up the Washington adventures to being an exhilarating but painful learning experience. As if making out a New Year's resolution list, she made plans.

I will lead a good, solid, stable life.

I will be a success in Small Town, USA.

I will forget all about Ross Rossiter.

Bob and I will get married, have two children—a boy and a girl.

I'll go to church every Sunday, teach a class, of course, write the society column for the newspaper.

I will entertain faculty members from the elementary school.

Bob and I will have weekend picnics and a week's vacation once a year, live in a frame house on a quiet street with shade trees and flowers beds and a garden in the summertime. We will go to the beach and maybe even Florida. Bob will be a good husband.

Beth reviewed her list and set her chin at a stubborn angle. That's what she'd do. She refused to let herself ask why she felt so unhappy about her well-laid plans.

&

After arriving home at dusk, Beth felt the kind of love and security she'd always felt with her parents. Aunt Catherine had called and forewarned them that Beth was coming and was not taking the news as well as they all had thought.

"We have loved you as much as we could our flesh-and-blood child," her mother said.

"You are our own," her dad added.

Beth nodded. She looked at her mother and father. In her heart and mind they were her parents. It was their influence, their environment, their teaching that made up her life. "You're my parents, and I love you," Beth replied.

Her mom and dad explained what they knew of the situation. Aunt Catherine had been pregnant. For some reason she didn't explain to them, she and the man would not marry.

Her mom explained that they couldn't have children. They'd had no idea they were infertile until after having tried to conceive for years. A doctor confirmed that it would be impossible for them to have children.

"We prayed fervently," Beth's dad added. "Adoption loomed large as a possibility. Then when this situation came up with Catherine and she talked of adoption, we knew God had listened to our prayers."

Her mom echoed what Beth had heard through the years. "You were our miracle child."

"We all decided you should be told when you were older," Dad said.

"The time never seemed right," Mom added. "I know this must be a shock."

Beth admitted that it was. "But it's all right. I'm glad I know. And it doesn't change how I feel about you." After a moment she added truthfully, "Or how I feel about Aunt Catherine. I'm blessed to have the love of all of you."

Soon, they were talking about her experiences and theirs during the time she'd been gone. After a couple of hours, her dad yawned.

"Are we boring you, Dad?" she asked and laughed. Looking at the clock, she saw that it wasn't quite ten o'clock. "I think I'll go see Bob."

❧

After finding a parking place at the back of the apartment complex where Bob lived, Beth went to the back door and knocked. No answer. She walked around to the front. The lights were all off. Maybe he'd gone to the store or something.

She returned to the back and went over to the children's playground next to a high fence. She sat in a swing beneath a maple tree at the side of the complex, next to a flower bed. The warm spring night displayed a bright moon, and stars lit the sky like diamonds. She moved her feet against the sand and watched the swaying shadows.

I'm back where I belong. Where people were honest and good and basic. Bob was steady and reliable. He never pushed her or pretended to care for her because of what he might get from her. He wanted the right kind of relationship based on Christian values, just as she did.

Yes, Catherine had been right. Beth had needed to see some of the world away from Henderson in order to appreciate the small-town values by which she'd been raised. Her parents, not her own? Yes, of course they were her own. They'd wanted her.

She remembered something she'd heard somewhere. A child had asked what it meant to be adopted. "It means," the mother had replied, "that you grew in your mommy's heart instead of her tummy."

Beth smiled at the sand beneath her feet. Her parents loved her. They knew how to give of themselves and of their love.

But she had gotten Aunt Catherine's love too. She'd always felt it. She loved her aunt. She loved her energy and ambition and all the exciting things that she did. In a million years, she wouldn't have suspected Aunt Catherine wanted her to know her birth father.

How strange that thought was. No one could have been a better dad than the man who'd raised her and loved her all of her life. She could not love another dad any more. Their love was complete. She had no doubt of that. If she had to have a birth father, she couldn't have chosen a better one than Jacobs.

Yes, being raised by her parents was a wonderful blessing for which she could thank God.

Maybe all this came out into the open in order to make her grow up, to appreciate her parents as she should. And to appreciate Bob. She would learn to appreciate his down-to-earth, commonsense approach to life. Yes, she'd wanted the frills, the ring to show off, the assurance Bob was truly hers—some sign. Now she realized she didn't need a symbol of his commitment. His wanting a lifetime with her was enough.

Wasn't it?

She didn't need visits to the White House, church with the president, candlelight dinners, moonlight walks, morning strolls beneath the cherry blossoms, time out to appreciate the beauty, talks about making the world a better place. Aunt Catherine was right; she had needed to see the world in order to make her appreciate where she came from, what she was—a product of her mom and dad. She could settle down now, have a humdrum life, and be glad of it. Be glad she'd known a man like Ross Rossiter.

Like her parents, Bob was basic and represented all that was good. She would devote the rest of her life to him.

A slight breeze caused a chill to race over her, and she realized her cheeks were wet. Why? Tears of joy—from having learned some of life's valuable lessons? She knew where she belonged. And with whom she belonged. Then why the tears? Maybe they were tears of revelation, of acceptance.

What had been the purpose of discovering Aunt Catherine was her birth mother? It didn't change anything. But she owed it to Bob to tell him. There was no need to keep such a fact secret.

Car lights appeared. Then Bob's car pulled into a parking place at the side of the complex a few spaces down from her own. She was about to get up and meet him when he opened the door and the dome light came on. He wasn't alone. He walked around the car as if to open the passenger door when the person inside opened it. She heard soft words and the light laughter of a woman. As they came into the light at the back of the building, Beth recognized one of the employees from Bob's school, Connie Jameson, a seventh-grade teacher.

Maybe they were working together on final exams or something. But. . .an English teacher and a history teacher? And not even the same grade level? Of course, they were friends. She'd seen Connie many times at school functions. They were friends. So, what was wrong with Connie visiting Bob late at night—although it wasn't all that late.

After all, hadn't Beth herself stayed in the house with a single man? But that was different. Jacobs was there. And servants. But hadn't she gone out—as friends—with Ross? And it was like Aunt Catherine had said—"It's proper. . .if you are proper."

Bob was a proper man.

She felt frozen as she watched the movement of Bob's hand touching the small of Connie's back as they walked toward the back door. But he was just leading her, wasn't he? It wasn't even as much as when Ross had put his arms around her shoulders and drawn her near, when he'd held her hand on Seventeenth Street, when he'd lifted her hand and kissed the back of it, when he'd leaned next to her ear and told her she was beautiful, when he'd put his hands on her shoulders and gazed into her eyes, when he'd said she was fabulous.

Suddenly Beth opened her eyes, and the blurry image revealed Bob and Connie had already gone into the building. She sat for a moment longer until she saw the light go on in his kitchen window. Were they going to have coffee—and talk about what Beth was doing in Washington—like friends might?

Beth rose from the swing, walked across the sandy play

area, and headed for her car.

&

The following afternoon Beth went to the school and walked into Bob's classroom a few minutes after three o'clock, when all the children would have gone. As she walked into the room, she noticed that Connie was there. Bob sat at his desk. Connie was opposite him, her hands on the edge of the desk.

"We'll have to try Table Rock again," Bob was saying to Connie. "Maybe it's warm enough to swim this time."

Connie straightened, looking surprised. "Beth. I didn't know you were back."

Bob looked more than surprised. He looked downright guilty. But he didn't rush to her and take her in his arms and express his delight at seeing her. "Did you just get in?"

"Late yesterday," she said, without saying she had gone to his apartment that evening.

Connie, whom she'd always thought rather drab, looked pretty. She had a glow about her, as if she too had had an adventure—as if something had come into her life.

Maybe it was just Beth's imagination or wishful thinking. Knowing Bob, and Connie, she believed the relationship between them was innocent. But it also made her realize that Bob would be all right without her.

"I have to run," Connie said. "See you two."

They all said, "Bye."

When Beth looked at Bob again after Connie was out of sight, he simply lowered his head to the papers on his desk and began to stack them and place them in his briefcase. Finally he looked up again, and as he did, Beth had a strange thought. Had his eyes ever sparkled when he looked at her? Or had they always held that distant, reserved look?

Had she ever really been in love with him? Or had she been in love with the idea of love? Bob was a fine man. The kind she was supposed to fall in love with, marry, and settle down with, and then together they would live happily ever after. Suddenly Beth realized her thoughts on the plane, and even before that, had been a fantasy.

There was no need to plan to have dinner and talk, or go and sit on her front porch in the swing as they'd done many times. She moved away and sat in a child's desk. "I was at your place last night. When you came home with Connie."

He took a deep breath. "You don't seem to be too upset about that."

She shrugged. "What could I do?"

"That depends on how strong your feelings are for me, Beth."

When she didn't answer immediately, he got up and closed his classroom door, then returned to his desk. He folded his hands in front of him, looking very serious. "Beth, I've always been afraid that we were mismatched. You were a cut above me in many ways. But you've been heading in the direction of Washington for as long as I've known you."

Beth could hardly believe her ears. Bob was giving her the brush-off?

"It was the patriotic programs, hymns, holidays that excited you most. Aunt Catherine was the ideal woman, with her career and political connections. You majored in journalism to be like your aunt. You minored in modern history, but not for the same reason I did—in order to teach," he said. "You simply loved studying about the development of our nation."

When had Bob become such a psychologist? Or counselor? It was as if she were a book he was reading, grasping its total meaning.

"You've prepared yourself for a future away from Henderson. And Beth," he said, with a pained look on his face, "I've read the articles and seen the pictures you've sent back from Washington that were printed in our paper. I've studied the pictures of you with those people and how you looked with them, and at them." He shook his head. "I knew you'd never be back—not in the same way."

Beth could not refute that. There was something to the saying, You can't go home again. She was here physically, but her heart was far away. She knew, as well as Bob, that she would return to Washington.

And being the nice, practical, polite Bob, he'd let her go without a fight.

twenty-one

Ross and Jacobs were deciding which of the senator's files should be kept and which should be discarded. Ross's words were ironic. "A few weeks ago I had my life all figured out. I knew what I wanted to do, and thanks to you, Jacobs, I knew what I needed to do to get there."

"Yes, we make our plans," Jacobs said. "But it is God who has the deciding vote. It is He who casts the secret ballot."

Ross had heard Jacobs talk like that before, but it had sort of rolled off his mind like water off a duck's back. Now, he took the words seriously. The person he'd been most close to, other than his dad, was Jacobs.

He thought of the letter he'd received that morning. An orphanage in Kosovo would be dedicated and named "Rossiter Orphanage" in memory of the senator. Would Ross name a date when it would be convenient for him to come and participate?

"I don't feel any inclination to return to Kosovo," Ross said.

Jacobs didn't comment but continued looking through files. Ross knew that humanitarian work, involvement in the needs of poor countries, was good for one's record if he planned to enter politics. There had never been any question but that he would enter the political scene.

Years ago, Jacobs had said, "You're a senator's son.

That's your foot in the door. Just as the sins of a father often pass down to their children, so do their accomplishments. Your dad is widely acclaimed and known as a good, honest man. You can step into those footsteps, Ross."

Those in the know thought Ross had a good chance of replacing his dad in the Senate after he retired. A few more years of public service, the right kind of publicity in the papers, personal appearances at the right places with the right people, and his future in politics would be assured.

Now, Ross felt nothing was assured. Did he even want to pursue a Senate seat? Politicians would say this was the right time to run, while sympathy ran high over the death of his dad. But Ross didn't have the heart to take advantage of his personal loss. The value of the Senate seat dimmed in comparison with the tremendous grief he felt at the loss of his dad. Ross tossed another file into the trash.

"What should I do?" he asked.

"Seek the Lord's guidance," Jacobs said. "I can't advise you on what to do. I can only advise you after you've made your decision."

"Jacobs, I know you might want to return to your home. But I wonder, would you consider staying on here? This big old house is kind of lonely."

"If you want me to," Jacobs said.

Despite their camaraderie, Ross knew they both were suffering. He'd lost his dad. Jacobs had lost his best friend of more than thirty years. Catherine McKelvey hadn't been around. Neither man had lounged in the library since Beth left. Her desk hadn't been touched. They didn't speak of her, although Greta's eyes spoke volumes, and her meals had lost a lot of their savor.

Maybe it was time to mention her. "I miss Beth," Ross said.

Maybe he shouldn't have mentioned her. He heard the pain in Jacobs's voice when he said, "I gained and lost a daughter. All in one day."

ૐ

Later that night, Ross couldn't sleep. He kept thinking of Beth.

They would have made a great team. They were compatible. But was he in love? Was it too soon to tell? How long should one wait before knowing? If she'd just come back to D.C., he could find out if this was love.

It had to be.

He'd never felt this way before. Was it love?

He could almost hear Beth say, "Pray about it."

Could he live for Christ like she did?

Pray about it.

For the first time in his life, Ross was taking a woman seriously. She'd invaded his heart. She'd touched his mind. She'd quickened his spirit. She'd made him see the beauty of politics in Washington and how it should be. That had given him motivation beyond simply trying to live up to some expected standard set by his Christian dad.

She'd made him come into his own. Think about his life, his abilities, and how life should be lived. She'd shown him the beauty of life. She'd stabbed his conscience, reprimanded his bad behavior. While lying in the dark, he felt like a light had been turned on inside, and he saw himself as he really was. Not as the fine upstanding political hopeful of the future.

He saw himself as self-centered, power-seeking, and willing to compromise even the faith of his father, the faith of his mother, the faith of his childhood. No, things were not always black-and-white in Washington. Many decisions had to be made when sometimes neither a yes nor a no seemed right. But he knew how his dad had handled such situations.

He remembered his dad talking with his mom over the table in the breakfast nook and how they'd end up holding hands and praying about a political decision. He'd heard his dad say that he wasn't sure how God was leading him to vote in a certain area, and he'd pray for guidance. Sometimes he wasn't sure he'd heard the voice of God. But he'd always let God know that he knew he wasn't smart enough to make those decisions on his own.

But me? Ross huffed. *I've assumed God was on my side, and I've felt I knew how to make decisions.* Ross now wondered if he'd thought such faith was hereditary. He knew better. He'd been taught by Christian parents. Maybe he should get on his knees and get things right with God. He slipped out of bed and knelt by its side, realizing he hadn't been on his knees since he was about six years old and staying in his grandparents' house. His grandmother had often said a man was tallest when he was on his knees.

He'd wanted to be taller. He'd said his prayers with his hands folded. When the prayer ended, he had straightened and tried to stretch himself. "Am I taller?" he'd asked.

"Oh, yes," his grandmother had assured him with heartfelt conviction. "You're definitely taller."

She'd smiled as if to say that he was the greatest. She'd

kissed him and pulled the covers up under his chin. She'd
left the night-light on for him. He had thought about
telling her she could turn it off since he was bigger. But he
thought again, and decided he'd wait 'til after the next
time he got on his knees. He'd be even taller then.

Now, as a grown man on his knees, he didn't feel as tall
as he had when he was a boy. He saw his weaknesses.
He saw his justification for what God called sin. No, he
wasn't terrible in the eyes of people. He wasn't as bad as
some of the mature political leaders. His dad's stand had
been his stand. Ross realized it was time for him to come
into his own and make his stand because of his own
beliefs.

"Forgive me, Lord, for going my own way. For giving
the impression that I'm just a chip off the old block. You
know and I know I'm not like my dad. I'm not half the
man he was. I can repeat his rhetoric. But there's a difference. His was from the heart. Mine is from having learned
the technique of what works with the public. I've done it
for me, God. Not for You.

"I've always believed Jesus is Your Son. I believe He
died on the cross for me and rose again. I thought that was
enough. But Jacobs says—or more important than that—
Your Word says I need Your Spirit in my heart. I'm asking
for it. I'm giving myself to You. Take my life and make of
it what You will. Show me what to do about Beth. What I
can do so that she doesn't get hurt. Amen."

Ross remained on his knees for a long time. Finally, he
rose. He evaluated himself. Did he feel taller?

No. His legs felt stiff. His knees felt sore. But he felt a
kind of peace in turning it all over to the Lord.

Back in bed, he asked, "God, did You send Beth here to show me that I'm not good enough?"

No! came the answer. *I sent Jesus to do that.*

twenty-two

"Mind if I join you?" Ross asked the next morning while Jacobs was having breakfast and his Bible lay beside him.

"Well, that's a new one," Jacobs said. "I never had anyone, in his own home, ask if he could join me at breakfast."

"No," Ross said, filling his plate. "I mean in devotions." Without looking, he knew Jacobs's look would be pensive, evaluating. The older man would stand for no nonsense when it came to his faith.

Ross took his plate to the table. "I'm serious, Jacobs." He told him about trying to commit his life to the Lord, the way he'd always known he should.

"But I don't have any great revelations," he admitted.

"Terrific!" Jacobs grabbed his arm. "Now there's room for the Lord to fill you up with His plans."

ᙇ

More than a week passed before Beth felt she was both facing the facts of her life and beginning to accept them. She had adoptive parents. She had a biological mother and father in Washington. She and Bob would never marry. She thought she loved Ross Rossiter, but she could not allow that relationship to grow, under the circumstances.

And finally, she admitted to herself and her parents that while she thought Henderson, South Carolina, was a wonderful town and had brought much to her life, she didn't belong there. She belonged in Washington, D.C. She wanted to live there and work there.

She shouldn't have been surprised that they understood her feelings. It was how Catherine had felt even when she was much younger than Beth. They had feared for a long time that Beth would want to leave South Carolina, but now that she was a grown woman, she had their blessing in whatever she chose to do.

"I'm returning to Washington tonight," Beth E-mailed Aunt Catherine. "May I stay with you?"

"Yes," came the reply. "Can I meet you at the airport?"

"I'll take a cab," Beth answered.

≥∎

Several hours later, Beth and her aunt Catherine stood in the foyer of the Capitol House, embracing, apologizing, and interrupting each other. Beth had a strong feeling this night would be much like the first night she'd spent there. The two women loved each other. There was no denying that.

And she was right. Long into the night, they talked. Beth admitted that she could easily fall in love with Ross. "But it can go no further."

"Why not, Beth? I've seen how he acts and looks around you. I know he cares."

"He's indicated that," Beth admitted. "But he's not a committed Christian. I can't allow myself to be seriously involved with someone who doesn't share my faith."

"Talk to him, Beth. He's a changed man since he lost his father."

Beth's heart leaped within her. No greater thing could happen to a person than to be totally committed to the Lord. People missed so much when they were halfhearted Christians. They risked so much when they didn't give God all of their lives so He could work in and through them. "How did that come about?" she asked.

"Gayle told me. She feels that her husband's death has caused Ross to think more seriously about every part of his life. That is the one factor that is getting her through this difficult time. Oh, we all know Ross is a good man, and he has been aware of Christianity all of his life. But he, like me, I suppose, has found it easy to fill life with activity, believing that God is good and everything's going to work out fine. Sometimes we forget that only if God is in control can things work our for the best."

"I'm so glad to hear that about Ross."

"But he's still learning and growing, Beth."

Beth nodded and smiled. "We all should be."

ه&

Jacobs and Ross were closer than ever, now that the senator had died. They needed each other. But their relationship had grown and deepened now that they shared their relationship with God. Jacobs had enjoyed being a political mentor to Ross, but being a spiritual mentor to a young man wanting to grow in faith brought a deep sense of joy to the older man that could only have come from God. It was a comfort to both of them during this troubled time of understanding that their lives were completely out of their control.

"I have a peace about this, Jacobs," Ross said, as they filled their breakfast plates. "I've turned my life over to God for His will to be worked out. But to tell the truth, I'm not too patient while waiting for an answer. I did as you suggested and E-mailed Beth, letting her know that I care for her, miss her, want her back here in Washington, but, most of all, I want her for what is best. If I'm not the best for her, I'm trying to accept that." He scoffed. "That's not easy."

"I know," Jacobs said. "Believe me, I've been there. But I also know that a relationship not built on a foundation of putting God first is doomed to failure. Love isn't enough. The relationship has to be endorsed by God."

"Well, save some for us," came a cheery voice from behind Jacobs.

Ross's face lit up as if a lightbulb had been turned on inside him. Jacobs looked around to see the two women in the world who could make his old heart beat like a drum.

Beth walked toward Jacobs with a softness in her eyes. He set his plate down and opened his arms to her. "Welcome back, Beth."

She moved back. "Well, I'm still under contract to write that column." She drew a grimace. "Unless I'm fired."

"I don't know," Jacobs said, frowning. "I'm only the editor. You'll have to ask the owner."

"On one condition," Ross said with such a serious look on his face, Jacobs wondered if Beth's return had shocked the young man so much that he couldn't think straight. His next words, however, made Jacobs more proud of him than he'd ever been in his life.

"On the condition," he said, "that you write the column without the disclaimer. Your advice that questioners turn their lives over to Jesus is now endorsed by the paper."

"I can live with that," Beth said softly.

Ross nodded.

The two of them seemed so lost in each other's gaze that Jacobs looked at Catherine, lifted his eyebrows, and picked up his plate.

Catherine smiled at the food and reached for a plate.

❧

"We all agree we're in a time of transition," Jacobs said

later, as the foursome enjoyed their breakfast and conversation. "Since I'm the elder here, let me impart a bit of wisdom."

He had Beth get a metal paper clip while he sought out Trudy for a pair of scissors and a toothpick. Ross got a paper towel, and Jacobs poured a clear glass two-thirds full of water.

The other three studied him closely.

He set the glass of water on the table. "This must be on a solid foundation to work," he said. "Now, watch." He dropped the paper clip into the water, and it fell to the bottom of the glass. Then he retrieved it. The next step was cutting a small square from the paper towel, which he then put on top of the water.

"Now," he said, "I'll put this metal paper clip on top of the piece of paper towel." He did. "See. It floats."

"Jacobs," Ross said bluntly, "I don't think this is the time for a scientific experiment."

"Oh, bear with me, Ross. Give me a little credit. After all, I have been your advisor for several years."

"Yes, and you could add how many times I messed up was when I didn't listen to you."

Jacobs grinned but said nothing. "Now, watch," he said. He took the toothpick and carefully poked the paper towel down from under the paper clip. The towel slowly fell to the bottom, but the paper clip continued to float.

While three pairs of eyes gazed at him with skepticism and questioning, he explained. "The molecules will work together to keep the paper clip afloat. If the water is disturbed—that is, if I shake this glass of water—the molecules will break apart, and the paper clip will sink to the bottom."

"Interesting," Catherine said, with a glance at him which plainly said, so what?

"The moral of the story is," he said, "that this same principle applies to a person in water. If you fight the water, you sink. If you remain calm, you float. Now, let this be an example to us. In this situation of ours, where we have difficult choices to make and the future is dim, we can stand on the foundation of faith. We can remain calm and stick together. Otherwise we're all paper clips, sinking."

"Neat," Beth said, as Ross quipped, "He's so profound. If this kind of illustration comes from my political advisor, maybe I'd better switch to dogcatching." He held up a hand. "Just kidding."

He and Beth smiled at each other.

"You are right, Jacobs," Catherine added. "Maybe we can come out of this walking on water."

Jacobs feigned disdain. "Maybe I should just retire."

"Now that brings me to a subject I'd like to discuss with you, Jacobs. If you've finished here, let's go into the library."

"Excuse us," Jacobs said, shaking the table as he rose, and the paper clip sunk. He'd never denied her any position on the paper she'd sought. Was she going to ask that he give the column to Beth—permanently—and that he step down so she could become editor?

❧

"Jacobs, I have an idea," Catherine said when the two of them reached the library. "I know Beth loves Ross and he loves her. I also know he's seriously considering running for the Senate. But you know as well as I that our past can rise up to haunt them. We need to turn all this into something positive."

"I've already shredded the investigative report," he said.

She shook her head. "Try again, Jacobs. The media hounds would sniff out that story before you could say boo. But we're her birth parents; we do have some kind of obligation." She moved to the edge of her seat, toward him. "Now here's what we're going to do."

After she told him her plan, Jacobs realized anew that Catherine McKelvey was indeed the master matchmaker. "Cat," he said, "have you ever considered running for president?"

She did a very strange thing just then. She had not smiled at him like that in more than twenty-six years. Nor had she looked at him with such a gleam in her eyes. A haunting melody invaded his mind, and he had an inclination to ask, "Could it possibly be, after all these years, they're playing our song?"

twenty-three

The wedding was beautiful. Beth's heart overflowed seeing the unrestrained love-light in the eyes of her birth parents as the small party gathered in the wedding chapel at Jacobs's church. Only close friends were invited. Beth's parents didn't feel it their place to travel to Washington for the event. The only attendants were Beth as maid of honor and Ross as best man.

As the vows were being spoken, Beth thought of her conversation with Aunt Catherine earlier. She had said the couple would have a reception after returning from their honeymoon and invite all of Washington. "But for now, just look in the morning's paper for the headline. The focus will not be on any scandal," she said, "but on the romance of the century."

"Oh, Aunt Catherine, you didn't do this for that reason, did you?"

"Oh, no. It just gave me an excuse to bring up the subject. I have loved Jacobs all of my life. He has told me his feelings for me have grown over the past few years, but he thought I had lost respect for him and wanted him to be nothing more than an acquaintance. He loves me, Beth."

"Yes, I can tell," Beth said.

As the "I dos" were being said, Beth was aware that her birth parents were getting married. God certainly could take any situation and work it out for good.

After Aunt Catherine and Jacobs had left for their honeymoon, Gayle Rossiter, Ross, and Beth returned to Rossiter House. Gayle would be staying in the house until the new couple's return. After his mother went up to her room, Ross asked Beth to stay for a moment. She could tell he wanted to discuss something serious.

He took her hands in his. "Beth, I'm not sure what God wants me to do with my life. I believe it may be service to our country in politics. That's a possibility. But while I'm waiting for God's answer, I've decided to make that trip to Kosovo for the orphanage dedication," he said. "The loss of my dad has had a profound effect on me. In one sense, I'm an orphan now. But I've had all these years with my dad. Some of those little kids don't even know what a dad is. Others have seen their dads or even their entire families literally blown apart. I really care, Beth."

She nodded. "I can tell you do."

"Beth," he said seriously, "would you like to go to Kosovo with me?"

For an instant she was taken aback. She'd hoped he'd take her in his arms and say he loved her. Once again, she was getting a bottle of perfume instead of a ring.

No, came another thought. *He's seeking God's will now, not his own.*

"I'll pray about it," she said.

≈

The following morning, after devotions with Ross and Gayle, Beth went into the library to work on the column. A piece of paper she didn't remember being on her desk lay right on top of a stack beside her computer.

She picked it up and read.

Dear Auntie,

I'm in love for the first time in my life with a beautiful woman who has changed my life and invaded my heart. I'm running for the office of husband. If you think this fabulous woman might be interested in becoming my wife, would she look over at the doorway and cast her ballot for the candidate?

With all my heart,

What is this? Beth asked herself. She flipped the paper over, then read it again. She looked at the doorway. Ross stood there. Then it hit her. She was speechless. Her heart was pounding so hard she was sure he could hear it. She wondered if her weak knees would even allow her to get up from her chair.

But she didn't have to. Ross came over to her and got on one knee. "Beth, I love you," he said. "For richer or poorer, sickness or health, till death do us part, will you be the First Lady of my life?"

"Oh, Ross, I love you too. And, yes, I'll marry you. On one condition."

"I've already prayed about it."

"Well, another condition," she said.

"What's that?"

"I get to pick where we honeymoon."

"Anywhere," he promised, standing and helping her to her feet.

Just before he enveloped her in his arms and she lifted her face to his, she answered, "Kosovo."

A Letter To Our Readers

Dear Reader:

In order that we might better contribute to your reading enjoyment, we would appreciate your taking a few minutes to respond to the following questions. We welcome your comments and read each form and letter we receive. When completed, please return to the following:

Rebecca Germany, Fiction Editor
Heartsong Presents
PO Box 719
Uhrichsville, Ohio 44683

1. Did you enjoy reading *Secret Ballot?*
   ❑ Very much. I would like to see more books
   by this author!
   ❑ Moderately
   I would have enjoyed it more if _____

   _____

   _____

2. Are you a member of **Heartsong Presents**? Yes ❑ No ❑
   If no, where did you purchase this book?_____

   _____

3. How would you rate, on a scale from 1 (poor) to 5 (superior), the cover design?_____

4. On a scale from 1 (poor) to 10 (superior), please rate the following elements.

   _____ Heroine   _____ Plot

   _____ Hero   _____ Inspirational theme

   _____ Setting   _____ Secondary characters

5. These characters were special because _____

   _____

   _____

6. How has this book inspired your life? _____

   _____

   _____

7. What settings would you like to see covered in future
   Heartsong Presents books? _____

   _____

   _____

8. What are some inspirational themes you would like to see
   treated in future books? _____

   _____

   _____

9. Would you be interested in reading other **Heartsong
   Presents** titles?   Yes ☐   No ☐

10. Please check your age range:
    ☐ Under 18   ☐ 18-24   ☐ 25-34
    ☐ 35-45   ☐ 46-55   ☐ Over 55

11. How many hours per week do you read? _____

Name _____

Occupation _____

Address _____

City _____ State _____ Zip _____

M·O·N·T·A·N·A

Montanans are legendary for their courage and willingness to take on challenges as big as the Montana sky. But the heroines in these four inspirational novels are ordinary people facing mountains of trouble. As the comforts of daily routine are threatened, they'll need to dig deep for a sustaining faith.

Set in the fictional town of Rocky Bluff, Montana, these four complete contemporary novels by author Ann Bell demonstrate the power of prayer, friendship, and love.

paperback, 464 pages, 5 ³⁄₁₆" x 8"

❤ • ❤ • ❤ • ❤ • ❤ • ❤ • ❤ • ❤ • ❤ • ❤ • ❤ • ❤

❤ • ❤ • ❤ • ❤ • ❤ • ❤ • ❤ • ❤ • ❤ • ❤ • ❤ • ❤

Hearts♥ng

Presents

__HP325 GONE CAMPING, *Gail Sattler*
__HP326 A TENDER MELODY, *Birdie L. Etchison*
__HP329 MEET MY SISTER, TESS, *Kristin Billerbeck*
__HP330 DREAMING OF CASTLES, *Gail Gaymer Martin*
__HP333 BEHIND THE MASK, *Lauralee Bliss*
__HP334 ESCAPE, *Kathleen Paul*
__HP337 OZARK SUNRISE, *Hannah Alexander*
__HP338 SOMEWHERE A RAINBOW, *Yvonne Lehman*
__HP341 IT ONLY TAKES A SPARK, *Pamela Kaye Tracy*
__HP342 THE HAVEN OF REST, *Andrea Boeshaar*
__HP345 THE PLAN, *Linda Lyle*
__HP346 DOUBLE TAKE, *Terry Fowler*
__HP349 WILD TIGER WIND, *Gayle Buck*
__HP350 RACE FOR THE ROSES, *Lauraine Snelling*
__HP353 ICE CASTLE, *Joyce Livingston*
__HP354 FINDING COURTNEY, *Birdie L. Etchison*
__HP357 WHITER THAN SNOW, *Yvonne Lehman*
__HP358 AT ARM'S LENGTH, *Gail Sattler*
__HP361 THE NAME GAME, *Muncy G. Chapman*
__HP362 STACY'S WEDDING, *Aisha Ford*
__HP365 STILL WATERS, *Gina Fields*

__HP366 TO GALILEE WITH LOVE, *Eileen M. Berger*
__HP369 A TOUCHING PERFORMANCE, *Ginger O'Neil*
__HP370 TWIN VICTORIES, *Cathy Marie Hake*
__HP373 CATCH OF A LIFETIME, *Yvonne Lehman*
__HP374 THE LAST COTILLION, *DiAnn Mills*
__HP377 COME HOME TO MY HEART, *JoAnn A. Grote*
__HP378 THE LANDLORD TAKES A BRIDE, *Kristin Billerbeck*
__HP381 SOUTHERN SYMPATHIES, *Andrea Boeshaar*
__HP382 THE BRIDE WORE BOOTS, *Joyce Livingston*
__HP385 ON THE ROAD AGAIN, *Gail Sattler*
__HP386 DANCE FROM THE HEART, *Louise Tucker Jones*
__HP389 FAMILIAR STRANGERS, *Gina Fields*
__HP390 LOVE ABOUNDS, *Ann Bell*
__HP393 BEYOND PERFECT, *Jennifer Peterson*
__HP394 EQUESTRIAN CHARM, *DiAnn Mills*
__HP397 MY NAME IS MIKE, *Gail Sattler*
__HP398 THE MUSHROOM FARMER'S WIFE, *Una McManus*
__HP401 CASTLE IN THE CLOUDS, *Andrea Boeshaar*
__HP402 SECRET BALLOT, *Yvonne Lehman*

Great Inspirational Romance at a Great Price!

Heartsong Presents books are inspirational romances in contemporary and historical settings, designed to give you an enjoyable, spirit-lifting reading experience. You can choose wonderfully written titles from some of today's best authors like Hannah Alexander, Irene B. Brand, Yvonne Lehman, Tracie Peterson, and many others.

When ordering quantities less than twelve, above titles are $2.95 each.
Not all titles may be available at time of order.

Heart♥ng Presents
Love Stories
Are Rated G!

That's for godly, gratifying, and of course, great! If you love a thrilling love story, but don't appreciate the sordidness of some popular paperback romances, **Heartsong Presents** is for you. In fact, **Heartsong Presents** is the *only inspirational romance book club* featuring love stories where Christian faith is the primary ingredient in a marriage relationship.

Sign up today to receive your first set of four, never before published Christian romances. Send no money now; you will receive a bill with the first shipment. You may cancel at any time without obligation, and if you aren't completely satisfied with any selection, you may return the books for an immediate refund!

Imagine. . .four new romances every four weeks—two historical, two contemporary—with men and women like you who long to meet the one God has chosen as the love of their lives. . . all for the low price of $9.97 postpaid.

To join, simply complete the coupon below and mail to the address provided. **Heartsong Presents** romances are rated G for another reason: They'll arrive *Godspeed!*